She was shaking with need

The surveillance video of the orgy had Amanda so turned on she was losing control. While her brain was disgusted and repelled by the sight of Hathaway with those women, her body was on fire.

"I'm here for you," Bolt assured her, his eyes full of questions.

"I don't understand what's happening," she whispered. She wanted to rip off her clothes and tackle Bolt like some kind of love-starved maniac.

Bolt gestured to the monitor. "This is like watching porn, Amanda. There's no shame in reacting—"

She shook her head, certain other forces were in play. "Hathaway is likely responsible for my sister's murder," she panted, unable to hold back the shiver of desire coursing through her, "yet my hormones are going wild."

He placed reassuring hands on her shoulders. "Just try to—"

At his touch, she was on her feet and flinging herself into his arms before she understood what she'd done.

She couldn't help herself. She needed sex. And she needed it with Bolt.

Dear Reader,

I'll be the first to admit—as a writer, I have two weaknesses. I like to write about the unusual, and I like to write about the incredibly sensual. Lucky for me, *Uncontrollable* allowed me to satisfy both passions.

In this story we come across a special perfume bottle, a bottle that inspires lust and first appeared in the *Essence of Midnight* anthology, written by Julie Kenner, Julie Elizabeth Leto and myself. The perfume bottle showed up again in Julie Elizabeth Leto's Harlequin Blaze title *Undeniable,* and once again it delivered on its promise.

Of course, I had to be different. In *Uncontrollable,* the villain gains control of the bottle, making my hero and heroine use their wits to counter the paranormal effects of the bottle's powers. And they have to be creative....

When I began to plot this story, I had no idea it would require so many love scenes. Not that it was a hardship. That's why writing is so much fun—I rarely know where my characters are going to take me.

I hope you enjoy the ride, too.

Susan Kearney

P.S. I love to hear from readers. You can contact me and read excerpts of my other books online at www.SusanKearney.com.

Books by Susan Kearney

HARLEQUIN BLAZE

SUSAN KEARNEY
UNCONTROLLABLE

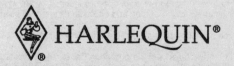

HARLEQUIN®

TORONTO • NEW YORK • LONDON
AMSTERDAM • PARIS • SYDNEY • HAMBURG
STOCKHOLM • ATHENS • TOKYO • MILAN • MADRID
PRAGUE • WARSAW • BUDAPEST • AUCKLAND

For my wonderful editor Brenda Chin.
Thanks for letting me take this story right to the edge.

ISBN 0-373-79189-5

UNCONTROLLABLE

Copyright © 2005 by Susan Hope Kearney.

This edition published by arrangement with Harlequin Books S.A.

® and TM are trademarks of the publisher. Trademarks indicated with
® are registered in the United States Patent and Trademark Office, the
Canadian Trade Marks Office and in other countries.

www.eHarlequin.com

Printed in U.S.A.

CLASSIFIED

For Your Information.
Read and Destroy.

The SHEY GROUP is a private paramilitary organization headed by Logan Kincaid whose purpose is to take on high-risk, high-stakes missions in accord with U.S. government policy. All members are either former CIA, FBI or military with top-level clearances and specialized skills. Members maintain close ties to the intelligence community and conduct high-level behind-the-scenes operations for the government as well as for private individuals and corporations.

The U.S. government will deny any connection with this group.

Employ at your own risk.

1

"HATHAWAY'S SO HOT, I'll never have to fake an orgasm again," bragged Francis Ledan, *Vogue*'s August cover model, about superagent Hathaway Balkmandy.

"He's hot all right," agreed another model, draped in a Versace gown beaded with delicate pearls and Parisian stitching. "Hathaway could keep the Statue of Liberty's torch lit permanently."

Hathaway. Hathaway. Hathaway.

Everywhere Amanda Lane turned in the ritzy New York ballroom, the legendary modeling agent's name spilled from the lips of famous women. So far this crush of A-list partygoers had made it impossible for her to approach the Hugh Hefner wannabe herself. Amanda bided her time and filled her crystal champagne flute from a silver fountain flowing with Dom Perignon. Far from being a Hathaway admirer, even she had to admit the powerful modeling agent sure knew how to throw a party. From the tuxedoed, white-gloved waiters serving exotic caviar on slivers of toast and cream-filled lobster canapés, to guests sumptuously decked out in designer couture, to Marc Anthony's live performance, the elegant ballroom was hopping beneath the Swarovski chandeliers.

Tapping one Brazilian Pappagallo shoe to the music, Amanda bided her time, secure in the knowledge that the .22 caliber tucked into her thigh holster might be small, but it was deadly. Almost as deadly as her wrap-style dress. Form-fitting through the bodice to show off her breasts, the chiffon nipped her waist then flowed gracefully but loosely over her hips, enhancing her figure. One of Hathaway's bodyguards speared her with a look. Amanda winked at him as if she belonged, as if she didn't believe that Hathaway had been the mastermind behind her sister Donna's classified formula ending up in the hands of a terrorist, as if she didn't believe Hathaway was responsible for her sister's murder.

Blend in.

Smile.

Flirt.

Amanda never forgot her mission. She was here to gain information about Hathaway's operations, and if clearing her sister's name and finding her murderer required her to wear sexy clothes and flirt, then she would act the siren.

She glanced toward Hathaway and, like the Red Sea parting on command, his coterie of sycophants, models and bodyguards parted for a moment, giving her a direct view of Hathaway's face. He didn't look like a monster, but was one of those men whose age was difficult to guess. With his rounded face and thinning hair, he could have been thirty or fifty. Amanda's extensive research had told her he was thirty-seven, and women adored him as much as he adored the models who milled around him. However, as Amanda and Hathaway locked gazes, she realized that her research had failed to prepare her for the searing crackle, a staggering snap of power, like the crack of a bullwhip, dangerous, deadly and oddly decadent, emanating from the man. But his disarmingly powerful stare wouldn't prevent her from forgetting she was here for justice.

Someone stepped between them, severing the weird connection. Amanda didn't wish to draw attention to herself and forced her gaze away, surprised by how difficult it was to ignore Hathaway's allure. Before she could analyze exactly what had just happened, she took a calming breath. Obviously seeing the man she believed responsible for her sister's death was upsetting. She must have read more into the exchanged glances than there was.

But no one else seemed to have noticed anything unusual. Guests chatted in groups, helped themselves to hors d'oeuvres and champagne. Marc Anthony finished the song and began another tune and Amanda's skitterish nerves settled.

But then her wandering gaze caught that of a scrumptious man exiting the gold-and-mirrored elevator and her heart sped up all over again. Amanda wasn't the kind of woman to judge a man by his looks, but then she wasn't accustomed to having a man with a movie-star face act interested in her. And there could be no doubting the man's interest. From across the ballroom, his gaze singled her out and caused heat to simmer low in her belly.

Good. She'd attracted an admirer. While she hadn't gotten close to Hathaway, she could hook up with someone and blend better into the party scene.

The stranger was single-mindedly shouldering his way through the crowd with an ease that belied his size. Sporting spiked, black-black hair, a square, oh-so-kissable jaw and a friendly boy-next-door smile, he approached with provocative intensity. Clean-shaven, he wore a navy Armani suit that matched the color of his eyes, a deep lavender shirt and a diamond ear stud.

When she lifted her chin, brazenly holding his gaze, he grinned, showing off charming dimples. Except for the slight crook of his bold nose, he was perfect. Totally yummy.

Fascinated by the man's apparent objective to reach her, she fortified her anticipation with a sip of champagne while keeping her gaze on him. The deepening warmth that drizzled downward from her stomach and caused a pleasant tingle between her thighs was a very physical reaction to the strong signals he radiated.

"Good evening." He spoke with a soft Southern accent, using a deep bass tone that would make any living, breathing women pay attention. "Did you come to the party alone?"

"Yes." She sipped her drink, enjoying herself and his direct approach. The singer's voice thrummed through her system but faded with the background crowd as she focused on the delicious-looking man.

"Then let me introduce myself. Bolt Tanner." His hand enclosed hers in gentle warmth and rough calluses. Whatever he did for a living required physical activity. But even before she'd shaken his hand, she'd known he worked out from the fit of his suit over powerful shoulders and from the way his slacks clung to his lean stomach and hips. Chatting couples around them passed by carrying his scent to her. Soap and shampoo, maybe a breath mint. No cologne. Just pure male heat.

She retrieved her hand, a little unnerved by her strong reaction to him. Never had she met a man quite so focused on her, and his intensity piqued her curiosity. Lately she'd barely noticed more than a guy's general height and weight, so she wasn't quite prepared for his stunning effect.

"Nice to meet you, Mr. Tanner." She hoped he wanted something interesting from her…like a kiss. A slow, sensual, seductive kiss. The kind that promised more. For him, she might even be willing to forgo her usual rule of getting to know a man for six months before sleeping with him and was glad she'd taken such care with her appearance tonight.

"Please, call me Bolt."

He lifted her glass from her hand, his fingers grazing hers and shooting an arc of electricity across her knuckles. Then holding her gaze, he deliberately turned the glass to sip from the exact spot her lips had touched, his maneuver smooth and intimate.

She tilted her head, eyeing him brazenly. "Bolt. You have an unusual name."

"Mother named me after her grandfather, a Florida fisherman who was struck by lightning three times and lived to tell the tale."

"You ever been struck by lightning?"

"No, ma'am." He chuckled. "Not until tonight when I saw you."

She laughed with him. "I set you up perfectly for that, didn't I?"

"As a matter of fact, you did." She hadn't expected him to agree, but his tone rang with sincerity. "But if it makes you feel better, you should know I haven't used that line before."

"Mmm." She let the comment slide. He knew exactly what to say and how to say it to put a woman at ease. "So are you one of Hathaway's models?"

"Now, why would you think that?" He pretended to be insulted, but clearly was not.

She cocked her head and assessed him frankly, letting him see her admiration of his handsome face, the high cheekbones, the predatory nose that contrasted with his easygoing smile. "You fit the part."

"So do you."

"Thanks." She'd expected him to angle for a compliment; instead he'd turned the tables. Obviously he had a quick mind behind those gorgeous blue eyes. And while a clever man always made her feel sexy, the chemistry between them sizzled. It was like an intoxicant bubbling through her veins.

As much as Amanda wanted to go with the flow, she didn't trust the over-the-top sparks. Something wasn't right. Something she couldn't define—not when her every female instinct urged her to see how far she could go.

Not about to ignore her well-honed instincts, yet not counting herself out just yet, either, she continued to play the game. "We both know I'm not tall or thin enough to work for Hathaway."

He glanced from her face and boldly dropped his scrutiny to her mouth, then lower. "You have plenty of…engaging features." At his appreciative glance, she could have sworn her breasts swelled. Her nipples most certainly tightened. He raised his eyes, clearly enticed by her response, and lowered his tone to a husky whisper. "I'll tell you a secret. I've always preferred a real woman. I don't know what Hathaway sees in these collagen-lipped models besides dollar signs."

"You know him?" she asked. Remembering she was here to scope out Hathaway was difficult while she conversed with such a striking specimen of masculinity. But she tried to focus on her goal and ignored the pulsing heat that beat like a go-get-him tattoo in her mind. She missed her sister too much to let lust sidetrack her.

"I only know Hathaway's reputation. While I admire his business acumen, his wretched taste in women has left the best one for me."

"Your name suits you," she teased. "You're as quick to strike as lightning."

"Quick?" Bolt glanced at the dance floor and shook his head. "I don't know about that."

"What do you mean?"

"Why am I standing here talking to you when I could have my arms around you? Would you like to dance?"

She licked her bottom lip, adoring the way his gaze followed her every little move. "I'd love to dance as long as you promise one thing."

"Not to step on your feet?"

She shook her head.

"Not to kiss you in front of all these people?"

Again she shook her head.

"What then?"

"Promise me that you won't keep your hands to yourself." Now, where had that comment come from? It wasn't something she would normally say. She might flirt. Yes. But she wasn't a tease and no damn way was she going to make love to this man tonight. But from what she'd just said, he had every reason to think otherwise. She hadn't drunk enough champagne to make such a mistake. What in seven blazes was wrong with her?

"Now, darling." His sexy grin widened. "You must be reading my mind."

"Is that so?" After he'd set her champagne flute on the tray of a passing waiter, she placed one hand on his shoulder and slipped the other into his. He swung her into his arms, and following his footwork came as easily as looking at him. In fact, when his hand settled on the bare small of her back, making her skin tingle, she didn't notice anyone else in the room.

Before she knew exactly who closed in on whom, her hips were snugly pressed to his, her breasts caressing his chest, as they danced. Every nerve in her body screamed to life, demanding she lure him away, then rip off his clothes. To distract herself from the incredibly hot sensations, she tilted back her head and looked at him. Up this close he was just as handsome.

Distract yourself.

"So what else is on your mind?" she asked, pleased she kept her tone breezy.

"Kissing you," he admitted and then his lips brushed hers.

Before she could think to pull away, pure molten heat singed her. Her lips parted in amazement. Sure she liked kissing, but this brushfire couldn't possibly be normal. When their mouths parted, she eyed him warily, wondering if he'd used some kind of sleight of hand to drug her drink. "Is this wise?"

"I don't want to be wise."

"Neither do I," she found herself admitting, speculating over when her objective had changed from blending into the crowd to satisfying her growing lust. She was ready to tackle the man on the dance floor.

What was wrong with her? She was acting just like those idiot models who couldn't seem to keep their hands off Hathaway. As they'd danced past the agent, she'd seen at least half a dozen women fawning over him, groping him. It was almost as if the air were saturated with an aphrodisiac.

Now that she considered it, the attraction between her and Bolt was way too strong, unusual, not just rare but downright weird. From the moment that elevator door had opened, he'd focused on her. He hadn't casually picked her out of the crowd, almost as if he'd intended for them to meet, but if that were the case, he hadn't been the least bit subtle, hadn't tried to hide his intentions.

The hair on her neck prickled. Was Bolt one of Hathaway's men sent to check her out?

Regardless of her raging lust, Amanda wasn't into one-night stands. She didn't pick up men. Not in bars. Not in ballrooms. Certainly not when she was undercover and wearing a gun that would give her away. And most certainly, she didn't sleep with the enemy.

She didn't care if every feminine and needy cell in her body wept and called her a traitor. Or if she had to take an ice-cold bath to soothe her burning flesh. After this one dance, she was out of here.

"So how did the meeting with Amanda Lane go last night?" Logan Kincaid, director of the Shey Group, asked Bolt, his tone conversational over the encrypted satellite phone call that had been rerouted through five countries before coming through the New York City line.

"Excellent."

Kincaid had arranged for Bolt to attend Hathaway's party for the express purpose of meeting Amanda Lane, but his boss hadn't told him why. But when a boss with Kincaid's reputation and brilliance made a suggestion, a man would be foolhardy to ignore it. During his former stint in the Agency, Bolt had heard rumors that Kincaid had been the driving force behind writing the code for the antimissile defense system before leaving the CIA to create the exclusive Shey Group, the private organization for which Bolt now worked. Kincaid's tentacles of power wound from the White House to the Kremlin to Beijing, but it was his loyalty to his men that endeared him to Bolt and fostered that same loyalty in return. He'd formed the Shey Group to take on missions the government wouldn't or couldn't touch, as well as lucrative private assignments.

Ex-Special Forces and ex-CIA, Bolt was no fool, so last night he'd followed his boss's suggestion to check out Amanda. The meeting had bowled him over.

Although he'd never been in love, he'd been involved several times, only to pick up and leave on a mission before things got too serious. Often when he was in the field, he thought about settling down one day and having a family, and when he imagined the fantasy, it was with a woman like Amanda, someone responsible as well as sexy and intelligent. He'd been pleased and surprised to discover a powerful attraction between himself and the woman, but he'd yet to understand why Kincaid had suggested they meet.

"Is she a client or under suspicion?" Bolt asked.

"Neither." Kincaid's clothing rustled and Bolt imagined his boss easing back in the leather chair of his penthouse office. "Amanda will be your partner for your next mission. You'll need her help to get near to the target. Conditions will require you to work close to her—very close."

"I have no problem with the last requirement," Bolt admitted. She suited him to a T. Oh, yeah. From her saucy expression to the sway of her seductive hips, she had kept him tossing and turning half the night with memories of their too-short dance. But when Bolt didn't work alone—as he had when he'd rescued a missing American executive from Columbian kidnappers—he worked with other members of the Shey Group, whom he trusted to watch his back. Bringing in Amanda was highly unusual. "Why pair me up with an outsider?"

"We have intelligence that Hathaway Balkmandy stole a precious antique. The Shey Group has been hired to retrieve it. You won't be able to get close to Hathaway without a female accomplice."

Bolt could accept that. He hadn't been back in the country long, but even he had heard how Hathaway constantly surrounded himself with the world's most beautiful women. The agent's face had graced the covers of *People* and *Time* always with a bevy of world-class models surrounding him.

"Why Amanda Lane?" he asked Kincaid. After meeting her, Bolt already felt she was special, but he wanted to know why Kincaid had chosen her.

"She's FBI, dedicated, intelligent and motivated." Kincaid briefed him on details that hadn't mattered until now.

Bolt caught a nuance in Kincaid's voice, one he was certain was there for him to pick up on. "She's motivated on a personal level?"

"Amanda's sister, Donna, was involved with Hathaway before she was murdered. Apparently Amanda's as suspicious as I am that Hathaway had something to do with it. While Amanda doesn't yet have proof, obviously her instincts are on target. I'll have Ryker send you both sisters' files."

"I look forward to reading them, sir."

"Donna was a brilliant chemist, involved in top-secret government research, who Hathaway lured from D&B Industries to model for his agency—an odd career change that I'd like you to find out more about."

For now Bolt would accept Kincaid's judgment that Amanda wasn't a loose cannon about to sabotage his mission because she recklessly sought revenge. Kincaid possessed superior insight into people and Bolt trusted his boss implicitly. If Kincaid believed Amanda could keep her cool, then she probably could.

Bolt leaned back in a chair of his temporary Shey Group acquired apartment. He appreciated the luxury of the butter-soft leather cushioning his large frame as much as he appreciated his Park Avenue view of the bustling city. Kincaid only supplied the best, employing the most up-to-date equipment money could buy. He leased top-notch quarters and the most skilled and trained men, operating on levels both large and small of scale, but always consequential in nature. Not too many men had a mind like his boss's.

The Shey Group team went to extraordinary lengths to complete their dangerous missions. However, Bolt had rarely found himself in quarters as richly appointed as this N.Y. penthouse, conveniently located across the street from Hathaway's suite. He couldn't wait to bring Amanda here and watch her take in the marble floors, museum-quality paintings, crystal chandeliers and gold faucets—such a far cry from his central Florida roots. He especially wanted to see her take in the bedroom. She could admire the furnishings while he admired her.

"Can you tell me more about the antique Hathaway stole?"

"Yes." Logan Kincaid paused, obviously taking care in his choice of words. "Sebastian Stone has hired us to retrieve an ancient and cursed Romany perfume bottle."

"Cursed?"

"Rumor says the perfume bottle was cursed by an eighteenth-century gypsy witch. Supposedly the bottle reflects the powers of an ancient gypsy shaman and now enhances the paranormal gifts of whomever owns it."

"So the legend makes the bottle valuable?" Bolt understood that historical objects took on value from the people who had once owned them, but Kincaid had couched his words with special care...as if the bottle still possessed unusual properties. But surely Bolt had misunderstood.

"Do you recall what happened to John Cameron?" Kincaid changed the subject abruptly.

"Yeah?" John Cameron had been caught and tortured during a mission, but the Shey agent had never yielded his precious data to his captors. Kincaid had rescued him and John had recovered, but that's all Bolt knew.

"During torture, John suppressed the details so deeply that not even he could recall them. We tried all the usual methods to help him unlock the secrets. They failed. Then I arranged for a psychic therapist to borrow the bottle to help unlock his memories. The therapist claimed the bottle was invaluable to retrieving the data."

"So the bottle helps memory recall?"

"The bottle enhances the powers its owner already possesses. If you don't have special abilities, it does nothing."

Bolt wasn't certain he believed in paranormal powers and wished for something more concrete to go on. "How does the bottle work?"

"Some say it's magic."

"Magic?" Despite his respect for his boss, Bolt couldn't keep the skepticism from his tone.

Kincaid remained calm. "I'm more inclined to believe there's some unexplained scientific reason for its unusual effects. Electromagnetics. Changes of polarity on the atomic levels. But it could be faith or smell or a gravity well or fairy dust. We simply don't know."

"From how far away can the bottle affect the owner?"

"We aren't certain, but think it must remain relatively close to project the full effect. Distance might weaken it. We do know Hathaway coveted the power and stole the bottle from Stone's brother-in-law, Nick Davis."

"Hathaway's wealthy. Why would he resort to theft?"

"He tried to buy it, but the bottle wasn't for sale at any price."

"Do we know if Hathaway's resold it?"

"All I know for certain is that Stone's sister and brother-in-law were crushed by the loss. He's willing to pay us a hefty price to retrieve the bottle. I've already sent you pictures."

"So the mission is to infiltrate Hathaway's life, find the bottle and recover it?"

"Yes. But," Kincaid continued, "I'd like to learn more about Hathaway. Since Donna's death, Amanda has been doing her own digging into Hathaway's background."

"He's dirty?"

"He's got his fingers in a dozen illegal Internet operations. He's hiding behind foreign corporations and subsidiaries so complex that no investigation could unearth all his maneuvering."

"Okay." Bolt didn't ask how Kincaid had acquired his information. His boss had friends in high and low places, and so many people owed him favors that his operatives knew he could pull strings if they got in a jam. If Kincaid said Hathaway had stolen the perfume bottle, then he had. If Kincaid said Amanda was digging into her sister's death, then she was. Due to the Shey Group's incredible resources, Kincaid had never fed Bolt incorrect data.

"Try to learn why women find it impossible to deny Hathaway Balkmandy anything he asks for. He may be using the bottle, intimidation, blackmail or bribery."

"Got it."

"Third. Keep an open mind."

Bolt had been expecting another concrete mission objective. Kincaid didn't typically give advice. He hired the best and expected his people to complete a mission as they saw fit. Bolt's fingers clenched the phone tighter and his gut clenched. "I don't understand, sir."

"Since we don't know how the bottle works, we don't know its limits, the extent of its effects. Unusual powers will make Hathaway a tough opponent." Kincaid's tone remained as casual as if he'd just claimed the sun was purple.

If anyone else had told Bolt that a perfume bottle had unusual powers he would have had difficulty controlling a laugh. However, his respect for Kincaid, who'd saved Bolt's life twice, was more than enough to curb his normal skepticism.

Bolt's mind broke into high gear and he quickly typed notes into his computer.

Antique perfume bottle.

Paranormal powers.

Before he attempted to infiltrate Hathaway's organization, he would research the subjects most carefully, assess the situation before deciding on the best way to proceed. He would read over Amanda's and her murdered sister's files. The entire operation required preparation and they all had to be on the same page.

"Sir, do we have any clue to where Hathaway keeps the perfume bottle?"

"None. And this is why I'm telling you to keep an open mind. Hathaway may *think* the bottle's powers come from perfume residue, but I've been told by a very reliable source that the bottle's properties exhibited themselves during a hundred-year span while the bottle remained sealed."

Despite his utmost respect for Logan Kincaid, Bolt's eyebrows rose. Clearly his boss actually believed the bottle enhanced paranormal powers and the skin on the back of Bolt's neck crawled. He'd seen Kincaid pull off missions no one else could. He'd benefited from the man's extraordinary foresight and his ability to think fast on his feet. Every single man who worked for the Shey Group would willingly take a bullet for him. So if Kincaid thought the bottle enhanced paranormal powers—Bolt would keep an open mind as Kincaid had asked of him.

Still, that meant the bottle wouldn't do Hathaway any good unless he had some paranormal power. "Is Hathaway known to have any unusual abilities?"

Bolt asked because Kincaid possessed resources he didn't. His boss could delve into black operations within the CIA through official connections, but he suspected the man could illegally tap into the Agency's encrypted programs as well.

"You mean besides the charm and charisma that women seem to find so appealing?" Kincaid asked, clearly thinking out loud, or perhaps he was slowly leading Bolt to believe what he needed him to believe to complete his mission. "You're missing the point."

Bolt thought again, recalling Kincaid's words. "Sir, are you suggesting this perfume bottle enhances Hathaway's powers with women?"

"That's exactly what I'm suggesting. And infiltrating his organization won't be easy. I believe Amanda's suspicion that Hathaway killed her sister is correct, but we don't know why. While your primary mission is to retrieve the perfume bottle, I'm interested in learning if and why Hathaway killed Donna. I wanted you to meet Amanda Lane and form your own impression whether you could work together before you were influenced by her impressive file."

Bolt didn't require Kincaid to spell out the rest. Amanda had left hurriedly and suddenly last night, but he'd had a sharp feeling she'd needed to put some distance between them. He hadn't missed her body's reaction just to his gaze, a man couldn't miss those hardened nipples teasing through her dress, and he couldn't wait to find out how she'd respond to some very direct stroking. He imagined she'd preen like a cat. Oh, yeah. Amanda Lane would work out just fine.

Since Hathaway surrounded himself with only female executives, a woman partner made sense. Bolt saw the merit in Kincaid's choice, but perhaps he felt that way because Bolt had always enjoyed women. Last year, he'd labored behind the scenes with a female Mossad agent. Although no sparks had flown between them, they'd developed a mutual respect that had led to friendship. Their successful mission had prevented terrorists from setting off a dirty bomb within the continental United States.

A man with three loving sisters, two aunts and a matchmaking mom, he was comfortable around the opposite sex and found them very appealing. Especially Amanda. She was a combination of tart sugar and sweet spice. In fact, just thinking about her roused both interest and excitement. His normal missions ran toward uncovering high-level criminal activity, preventing terrorism and recovering kidnapped corporate executives—not retrieving a perfume bottle from New York's top modeling agent. His current mission, while danger- ous, was more upscale and had the added bonus of working with a very delectable woman partner.

"The final decision of whether to accept Amanda as a partner is still up to you."

"Appreciate that." But as Bolt ended the call, he'd al- ready made up his mind.

And reading her file only confirmed his impressions of her. Dedicated, motivated, smart, she was a terrific choice for the mission. Like all FBI agents, she had specialized training that would help her deal with the unusual circumstances of this mission. Besides, her background had already been thoroughly checked out and he approved of her skills. Though it wouldn't sit well with some of the macho men he often worked with, it didn't bother Bolt that she was probably a better shot than he was. A partner who could shoot with skill might save his life as well as her own. Based on her file, though, he suspected she'd never fired her gun at a mov- ing target.

He glanced at her picture, drawn to the secretive smile on her pretty mouth. But it was her eyes, the color of the autumn sea, that grabbed him, dark green eyes that swirled with hidden recesses and untold depths in which a man could willingly become lost.

Oh, yeah. He could definitely enjoy working with a partner like Amanda Lane. Now all he had to do was convince her that she wanted to work with him.

2

SINCE DONNA'S DEATH seven months, five days and three hours ago, Amanda had immersed herself in work. Her heart ached as if fate had chewed it up and spat it out. Moments when she could combine business and pleasure, like last night at Hathaway's, were rare. Although friends and colleagues had suggested she take time off, she couldn't handle empty hours. Not when her thoughts always converged on the loss of her sister. Although they hadn't been as close over the last months, when Donna had worked for Hathaway, the connection they'd established after their parents' deaths had made them much tighter than most siblings. Guilt weighed on Amanda that she hadn't made more time for Donna during those final months. Perhaps if she'd visited her sister in New York, she might have somehow prevented the tragedy.

Consumed by grief, Amanda kept herself focused and busy. With her mind occupied, she tried not to dwell on the fact that with Donna gone, she was the last surviving member of her family.

She'd attempted to bury her grief by burrowing

through piles of paperwork. Her job was to decide which cargo to search aboard ships and trains in order to discover any illegal imports that could threaten the safety of U.S. citizens. When she finished with her own files, Amanda used her FBI resources to investigate Hathaway Balkmandy, the last person to have seen Donna alive.

That's why she'd wrangled an invite to his party last night. She'd intended to get to know the man, watch the way he operated. But between his bodyguards, the models constantly surrounding him and the very distracting Mr. Bolt Tanner, she hadn't accomplished her goal. Failure didn't sit well on Amanda's shoulders. In fact she prided herself on working hard enough to make sure she achieved success. And while she'd have liked to blame Bolt, she'd been a willing participant in their flirtation.

And what a flirtation it had been. She'd paid for it with a cold shower followed by a sleepless night. Even now, just the thought of him caused a breathless hitch in her lungs. The vibes between them had been powerful. Uncontrollable.

But attending Hathaway's party had left her at square one. According to the police report, Hathaway had sent her sister to model at a fashion show, but Donna had never arrived. Her body had been found in a Dumpster. The coroner's report stated she'd suffered one bullet to the head.

Amanda didn't feel one bit better knowing Donna hadn't suffered. She was feeling enough sorrow and hurt for them both. Despite typical sister disagreements, she and Donna had been close. And now they would never speak again. Amanda would never again have the pleasure of hearing Donna's passion for life, never again look forward to her phone calls and visits. The sharp grief seemed to have taken up permanent residence, leaving a slicing pain inside her. And when the grief lessened, anger swept in. Especially after the rumors started. Ugly rumors that rubbed Amanda's wounds raw. No way would her brilliant sister sell secrets to terrorists, but Amanda was unable to explain how Donna's top-secret formulas for the government and D&B Industries had ended up on a terrorist's computer. When the man had been captured, the evidence had been right there on his hard drive.

When her intercom beeped, Amanda was so deep in thought, she jumped and the file she'd been holding slid to the floor. Scrambling on hands and knees to pick up the scattered papers, she heard her secretary announce, "You have a visitor."

"No visitors," Amanda said. But of course, her secretary, Kelly Bennito, couldn't hear her since Amanda couldn't activate the switch from the floor. No matter. She'd just send her visitor away. Months ago, her friends had given up their attempts to get her to leave the office before midnight. She'd overheard colleagues talking about her mental state behind her back, but Amanda didn't care.

So what if she had dark circles under her eyes? So what if she'd gained ten pounds from nervous eating? It wasn't as if she had a man in her life. Last night and her attraction to Bolt Tanner had been an aberration. An inexplicable anomaly that she now had under control—especially since she had no intention of seeing him again.

Her office door opened, and for a moment they just stared at each other. She looked up to see Bolt Tanner.

"Bet you didn't expect me to show up here," he finally stated.

"You called that right."

Shocked by his presence in her office, she picked up the last of the spilled papers, using the time to gather her thoughts. How had he found her? She hadn't told him where she worked or even that she was an FBI agent. And why did he have a thick file stamped Classified in his hand? Then she recalled her impressions from last night, not only the passionate ones, but her feeling that he'd intended to meet her before the elevator doors had opened and he'd first seen her. So he'd planned the meeting. But why?

He strode toward her looking as good in jeans and a khaki jacket as he had in a suit. When he held out his hand to help her to her feet, she didn't hesitate. "Why did you seek me out last night?"

Surprised she sounded so normal, she nevertheless braced against the pulse drumming in her ears. But when he released her hand, she didn't walk around to her chair and put distance between them. Instead she spontaneously decided on a different tack. She swung a hip onto her desk, crossed one knee over the other and let her shoe dangle provocatively off her rocking foot, enjoying the sight of him checking out her legs almost as much as she'd enjoyed their dance last night.

When he realized she'd caught him staring, he didn't even have the grace to look sheepish. Instead his bold blue eyes captured her gaze and he held up the thick document. "You're much better looking than the picture in your file."

"Thanks."

Now this was interesting. He must have a higher security clearance than she did to have access to her file. Yet, he didn't act like FBI. There was an inbred cockiness to this man, a certain seductive savoir faire that came from a combination of education, training and breeding that money couldn't buy. His kind of scrumptious and sexy confidence took intelligence and experience and implied a manner of operating outside the box. Another woman might have thought him arrogant, but Amanda was beguiled by his charm. She'd always appreciated men with extraordinary skills—and this guy had them in spades. Last night, she'd been thinking mostly with her hormones, no doubt due to his enticing charm. That she hadn't ended up in his bed had been a minor miracle.

But now that she was out of the party mood and her head was cleared of champagne, she took a harder look at him. The calluses on his hands suggested he was skilled in hand-to-hand combat as well as firearm drills, and he fascinated her by allowing her to see exactly what he wanted her to see—and no more.

She couldn't read below his surface and that, more

than his eye candy exterior, intrigued her. "Surely you didn't come here to suggest I should update my picture? Did you expect me to forget that you didn't answer my question about why you arranged for us to meet last night?"

She wished he'd get to the point of this visit before her curiosity made her say something foolish—like *if you aren't married, I'm interested.* She refused to glance at his hand to see if the ring he hadn't worn last night was back on for his day job, because a man like him would notice. And she wasn't yet certain if she wanted him to know the surprising effect he had on her.

Her attraction wasn't simply chemistry. Sure she liked the outside package, but she wanted to know what kind of man was behind the pretty clothes, perfect hair and charming voice.

"Are you always so good at small talk?" he teased, his lips turning up again in an easy smile.

She licked her bottom lip and quirked an eyebrow. "Small talk bores me."

He chuckled, his laughter heating up his blue eyes. "I sought you out last night because you're going to be my new partner."

BOLT WATCHED AMANDA'S dark-green eyes narrow, a corner of her mouth twitch, dishing out amusement along with her obvious skepticism. "My work doesn't require a partner."

Bolt had been pleased with her skills when he'd read her file, but nothing could compare to the captivating picture she'd made in his arms last night. He'd had to restrain himself when his lips had brushed hers. And now his every instinct told him Logan Kincaid had made the right choice when he'd chosen Amanda Lane to work with the Shey Group.

Last night he'd seen one side of her, now he was seeing another. She was as quick to put unrelated facts together as she was light on her feet. FBI agents tended to be by-the-book kind of people. But Amanda had attitude in spades. From the tilt of her saucy chin to her angled hip to her rocking foot, her body language told him that although she might still be grieving for her sister, she was by no means broken. Clearly, top to bottom and inside to out, Amanda Lane was a fighter. One with curves that made his fingers itch to stroke them.

Although skinny women were all the rage, Bolt preferred a woman whose bones didn't make him wince when he held her. And Amanda's proportions were exactly suited to his taste. But more important than her attractive appearance was her self-assured outlook. She wasn't one of those women whom he saw too often in law enforcement, one who wanted to show she was better than a man. She challenged him, but in a feminine way that revealed she was confident in her own skin and had nothing to prove to herself or to him.

He watched carefully as he revealed the mission. "I'm going after Hathaway Balkmandy, and I thought you might be interested."

"What gave you that idea?" Her nostrils flared. Her shoulders stiffened but only another professional would have picked up on her reaction. Oh, Amanda was cool under stress, perfect for the mission. "And who the hell are you, Mr. Bolt Tanner?"

"I work for the Shey Group. My boss has asked your boss to e-mail you a letter of reference. If you check your computer—"

"I'll do that." She leaned over her desk, brought up her e-mail and her eyes widened. "This came straight from the director of the FBI."

"The Shey Group works closely with the government."

"I've heard of Logan Kincaid. The man's a legend. However, I wasn't aware he'd left the Agency." She read the letter quickly and glanced up at him. "You work for the Shey Group and Kincaid?"

"Yes."

"Why are *you* going after Hathaway?"

"I have intel that Hathaway stole an invaluable antique perfume bottle, and our client's paying us to recover his brother-in-law's property."

She frowned, her pretty lips forming an enticing pout. She really had incredible lips, full, natural and brazen, and he couldn't help wondering if she would taste as sassy as she acted. Working with a partner always had advantages, brainstorming and taking turns at surveillance during the inevitable lulls in action. His last mission had involved sitting through desert sandstorms and waiting for an urgent radio contact that had never come. Usually Bolt played cards or talked sports to kill the downtime, but his mind kept leaping to all the wonderful things he and Amanda could do together, like long seductive kisses that led to exploring her enticing curves. Oh, yeah. This time he'd lucked out, drawing an interesting mission and one hot partner.

Rocking her slender foot, the back of her stylish shoe tapped her sexy heel, which was gloved in a skin-toned stocking. "The FBI isn't in the business of recovering stolen items."

"It is now." He reached into his pocket and presented her with a second letter from the FBI Director, offering Amanda Lane's service to the Shey Group. "But only if you agree. I don't work with unwilling partners."

She scanned the official letter, then glanced at him, her curiosity making her eyes sparkle emerald-green. "You came to me because of my sister, didn't you?"

He nodded.

Her captivating eyes also revealed a shadow that hinted at pain. "If we're going to be partners, you should know that I believe Hathaway killed my sister, and I'm going to search for evidence to prove it."

"Tell me about your sister." He'd read the file, memorized the classified information. Her sister had had a genius IQ and according to her colleagues had an insight in her field that allowed her to think creatively. But he wanted to hear Amanda tell him about Donna in her own words.

"Before Donna went to work for Hathaway, her last project was for D&B Industries. My sister was brilliant, one of the best in her field and could write her own ticket among dozens of defense contractors that constantly courted her," she stated without emotion. "The top-secret chemical formula she'd patented was specially formulated paint to allow ships and planes to avoid radar."

He found it interesting that she recited the facts so dryly when her sister had obviously meant so much to her. Almost as if she allowed any emotion to escape, she'd open a floodgate. "Go on," he urged.

"The classified patent was discovered on a captured terrorist's computer. I can't do anything to bring back my sister, and Donna can't defend herself from the accusations that she sold out and betrayed our country, but I can work to find her murderer and clear her name."

"So how's it going?"

"Every clue I've followed leads to a dead end. After months of slow and painstaking research, I'm no closer to knowing how Donna's formula got into terrorist hands than before I began. And I'd like the SOB who killed her placed behind bars for life."

"Not dead?"

"Too easy. I want him to suffer." Her tone was hard, flat, determined. And behind every word was raw pain.

Bolt wanted to reach out and pull her into his arms but he hadn't earned that right. And she didn't want comfort. She wanted revenge. He understood. If anyone ever harmed one of his sisters, he'd feel exactly the same way.

"You and Donna were close?"

Amanda swallowed hard and nodded. "After our parents died in a skiing accident, I raised her."

More details were in the file. Amanda had used their

parents' life insurance to put herself through school. Then she'd worked two jobs to pay for her sister's college and graduate school. She hadn't lost only a sister. Donna had been like a daughter, as well. And now Amanda was the last surviving member of her family.

But she was no longer alone. She had him. She had his help and the Shey Group's as well. And he liked her up-front honesty enough to give her the same in return. "I have no problem with your agenda as long as it doesn't interfere with mine."

She didn't hesitate. "Then I'm in."

That she made her decision so quickly impressed him. Either she knew a hell of a lot more about the Shey Group than she'd let on, or she was a risk taker after his own heart. Either way, he wanted to know her better. "I understand you've been doing your own research into Hathaway."

She frowned at her computer. "My system's been hacked by the Shey Group?"

"I'm not sure how we came by the information." That kind of data was on a need-to-know basis. So his response wasn't a lie, but he suspected she was correct. Ryker Stevens was a computer specialist for the Shey Group and Bolt had seen him perform miracles. The man had a knack for breaking encryption systems that couldn't be broken. He'd once tapped into a Chinese system to find a launch code against Taiwan, allowing Bolt to convince a diplomat that he needn't start a war.

She crossed her arms under her breasts, her tone firm. "If we have an FBI leak, I need to report it."

Usually the Shey Group played by the rules, but sometimes they used superior technology to find out what they needed. In her case, he really didn't know how they'd come by the intel, but he tried to reassure her. "If you had a leak, it was authorized." He shifted in his seat. "What can you tell me about Hathaway?"

Amanda hesitated, then apparently let go of her suspicion of the Shey Group with a delicate shrug. "He's wealthy, charming and he's close to the models he represents, accompanying them on many shoots. He knows all the right people and is on every New York City A-list. There's not a whiff of scandal attached to his name, but some hard digging has led me to find that he might be into Internet pornography. Yet he hides behind so many corporations I can't untangle or prove anything. What bothers me most, though, is his reputation with women."

"What about it?" he prodded, pleased to see that she'd dug up some dirt on Hathaway on her own. Amanda seemed to be everything the FBI claimed. She was smart, persistent and intuitive. Looking at her, he'd never have suspected she was directly behind preventing the importation on an arms cache into the metropolitan area. She'd even disobeyed her direct superior's orders and led a field team to stop the train from leaving the depot, earning her a well-deserved promotion.

Exasperation clouded her eyes. "I don't understand why my sister was attracted to Hathaway."

"What do you mean?"

"Donna had just gone through a nasty divorce. She'd

sworn off men. Then Hathaway makes an offer to represent her and she not only gives up a career she adored and the respect of her colleagues as head chemist at D&B Industries, but she falls for the guy."

"Your sister and Hathaway were in a relationship?"

"A one-sided one. He still dated lots of other women. And my sister, who hated cheating men after an ugly situation with her ex, put up with Hathaway's roaming ways."

Amanda sounded so puzzled that Bolt gathered her sister was not the kind of woman to fall so suddenly, so hard. Amanda's assessment supported Kincaid's bizarre theory that Hathaway might have an unnatural hold on women.

"Could Hathaway have been blackmailing her?" he asked.

Amanda shook her head without hesitation. "She couldn't have faked that kind of happiness. Not to me."

"I don't understand."

"The last time I spoke to my sister, she was almost euphoric. Giddy. Elated. She actually told me that Hathaway might be the love of her life. If Hathaway had been blackmailing her, she wouldn't have sounded so delighted."

"I agree." Still, he intended to examine Donna's checkbook and credit card statements as well as her phone calls for anything unusual. Perhaps she'd been lying through her teeth to protect Amanda. While Amanda had probably already checked her sister's financials, and in truth was more likely to notice a suspicious detail than he was, she wasn't looking for the unexplainable.

Amanda raised her gaze to him. "What aren't you telling me?"

Her instinct that he was holding back on her was dead-on. Although he'd planned to wait until later to tell her about the paranormal properties of the perfume bottle, he repeated what Kincaid and the files had told him.

Surprisingly Amanda didn't throw him out of the office. She listened, considering the possibilities of the gypsy-cursed antique bottle's unknown properties with a seemingly open mind. She didn't mock him. She didn't say much at all about her belief or disbelief in the paranormal. And then she took the possibilities farther than he ever could have, running the paranormal idea in a new direction.

"You know, my sister only actually modeled for Hathaway twice. Do you suppose that was a cover?"

"For what?" He had no idea where she was going, but she'd heard him out. Now it was his turn to listen and give her ideas the same consideration.

However, even now, his concentration was divided between the interesting conversation and her sexy calf. That she kept drawing his eyes to her leg by pumping her foot as she spoke had him struggling to keep his gaze on her face. Not that looking at her face was exactly a hardship. She'd used just a touch of mascara to enhance her lashes, and the high gloss of her lips as she spoke held him entranced.

"Donna was a genius at chemistry. Suppose Hathaway really hired her to examine the bottle?"

"Your file didn't say *you* were brilliant." His compliment was genuine. Her idea shot him into a totally new direction. He'd never made the connection between the bottle and Donna's expertise as a chemist. "But how exactly could your sister's skills help Hathaway?"

"I'm not sure." Her brows narrowed. "Maybe Hathaway hired Donna to find out how the bottle worked. If there was a perfume residue or a scent, maybe he'd want her to duplicate the formula. Or suppose there were drugs in the bottle, Donna could analyze the formula and replicate it." Amanda threaded her hand through her hair. "One thing I know for certain. My sister would never betray her country. While I can't explain how her classified formula ended up in Pakistan on a terrorist's hard drive, I do know she would never have given terrorists her work—one of her best friends died in the World Trade Center."

He whistled softly at her implication. Kincaid was going to love this angle. "You think *Hathaway* might be responsible for your sister's work ending up in terrorist hands?"

Amanda's voice hardened with determination. "I can't prove anything criminal about that man's activities, but I will. Instinct tells me Hathaway is at the bottom of this mess."

Her eyes dropped but not before he saw her despair and frustration. He stood and placed a comforting hand on her shoulder. "We'll find a connection."

"I've been searching, but I haven't found one link."

"Perhaps you haven't looked deep enough."

"Maybe. That's why I agreed to become your partner," she said and he didn't miss her message.

She drilled him with a stare as if her determination could make him forget their flirting last night. But nothing would erase their first meeting from his mind. She had branded him with her sparkle and wit. But he didn't let his thoughts seep into the conversation and tried to stay as businesslike as she was.

"How long will it take you to wrap up things here?" He gestured to her desk.

She slung a jacket over her shoulder, picked up an overnight bag on wheels that she apparently kept packed for sudden trips. "I'm ready now. Where do we start?"

He'd expected to have to sweet-talk her into working with him. That she didn't need convincing or more explanations told him she was one determined woman. Good. "The plan is to insert you undercover into Hathaway's organization."

"So that's why you need me. Hathaway only hires female executives."

Amanda didn't seem to mind that her double X chromosomes had won her the job as much as her excellent FBI credentials. In fact, convincing her to work with him had been almost too easy. Yet he wasn't about to complain, although a bit of guilt stabbed him that he hadn't told her how Hathaway might be employing the bottle, especially after she'd been so honest with him.

"Before we try to insert ourselves into Hathaway's organization, some surveillance is in order."

"What do you have in mind?" she asked, slipping into her gun's shoulder harness as easily as another woman would have slung a purse over her shoulder. Then she put her jacket on over the top and grabbed the handle of her bag.

"I'd like to watch him at work and at home before we come up with a plan." Bolt opened her office door for her and they strode toward the street and his car. "Are you okay with leaving your vehicle here?"

"No problem. We have a security guard and the lot is fenced. How long can I expect to be gone?"

"Until we find and steal back the perfume bottle."

She shook her head, a lock of hair falling over one eye. "In other words, you have no idea."

He chuckled. "I suppose that's one way of looking at it."

"I'll need to make a few arrangements."

He guided her to his car, opened her door, and she slid into the front seat, giving him another view of her terrific legs. By the time he'd placed her bag in the trunk and walked to his side of the car, she'd reached for the seat belt and had snapped it across her lap.

He drove into the city, but they didn't have much opportunity to talk. She had her cell phone to her ear, making arrangements with a neighbor to feed her cat, bring in the newspaper and mow the lawn. Personal business taken care of, she spent the rest of the trip distributing her case files to assorted colleagues.

He admired her efficiency. Bolt knew none of his sisters could have switched gears so fast. Lacy would have chewed him out royally if he'd made her leave for even one night without her makeup bag. Darlene would have created a huge fuss, then insisted on shopping to find the right outfit. And Melody would have simply refused to leave home.

He glanced at the bulge under Amanda's arm. But then his sisters didn't wear a sidearm, either. Until now, he'd never considered that packing a weapon could be sexy. When she paused between phone calls, his curiosity got the best of him. "Were you armed last night?"

"Of course."

While she dialed and spoke to yet another colleague about a batik shipment from China, he wondered exactly where on her person she'd hidden a gun. The thin-strapped gown and form-fitted waist hadn't left her many options. As he thought of all the fun a search could have been, he couldn't recall ever looking forward this much to a mission.

Right now, Amanda was all business, but sooner or later—out of necessity—she'd have to turn her attention to him, and he couldn't help wondering how she would handle herself.

3

AMANDA HAD FINALLY finished clearing her schedule when Bolt was parking the car. After removing her bag from the trunk, he escorted her from the underground parking garage into an elevator that rose into one of the most exclusive buildings in the city. The bottom block was retail space but above were luxury suites.

"Is this place yours?"

Bolt shook his head. "Hathaway lives and works across the street. The Shey Group leased this space for the duration of the mission."

She glanced from a lavishly framed mirror back to him. "Must be nice working in the private sector."

"There are advantages."

He grinned a relaxed, charming smile that put a new arc of electricity between them. She allowed him to lead her through an impressive marble and gold wallpapered foyer. When he stopped to unlock mahogany double doors flanked by beautiful silk palm trees in oriental porcelain pots, she realized the suite had its own private entrance.

So far, Bolt had been the perfect gentleman and although the attraction from the previous evening still hummed between them, she now felt back in charge of her emotions. The out-of-control zinging current that had made it so difficult to tear herself from him last night had significantly diminished. She still found him handsome and charming. But her response was more measured, more normal, so much so that now she wondered if she'd imagined how on edge she'd been. First she'd exchanged that odd look with Hathaway, and then she'd met Bolt and her attraction to him had been uncontrollable. Perhaps her friends were right. She did need to get out more.

Reassured she wasn't walking into anything she couldn't handle, Amanda strode through the double doors proud that she didn't stop to gawk. Still, she couldn't help but appreciate the original oil paintings hanging on fourteen-foot-high walls. Or the decadent multilayered, two-toned carpet beneath her feet that was so plush she wanted to kick off her shoes. Or the pleasant sound of the cascading fountain, complete with live fish. She sniffed and even the air smelled crisp and clean, scented with a half-dozen jade vases of exotic flower arrangements.

"We're working surveillance from here?" she asked, marveling how easily Bolt appeared to fit into such luxurious surroundings. The high ceilings suited his tall frame. And the lush furnishings set off his easy stride that reminded her of a panther, light-footed yet ready-to-spin and face danger head-on at the first sign of trouble.

He'd picked up her bag by the handle, careful not to allow the wheels to dig into the carpet, and led the way down a wide hall with a stormy seascape mural. He opened a door into a lovely bedroom with a polished cherry king-size sleigh bed covered by a spread embossed with a rich-threaded design of golden daisies.

"How do you like your new room?" he asked.

"And you'll be staying…where exactly?"

His eyes twinkled. "In a separate bedroom…until you decide otherwise."

She hadn't missed the way he'd said *until* and her heartbeat sped. As if their coming together was already destined. While she liked confidence in a man, Bolt was too good at guessing how to push her buttons. Deciding to ignore the comment for now—though it would probably haunt her during the night—she opened a door to a walk-in closet.

"It's larger than my entire bedroom."

"Yeah. It's difficult to imagine having that many clothes, isn't it?"

She liked that even though he appeared at ease in the wealthy surroundings he didn't try to pretend that he belonged here any more than she did. "Your parents weren't wealthy?"

He shook his head. "But we weren't poor, either. Mom's a teacher. Dad owns his own heating and air-conditioning business. We were comfortable, but taking a vacation on the Gulf of Mexico was a big deal."

"Where are you from?"

"Central Florida. Orlando."

She opened her bag and hung up her extra suit, which looked ridiculously lonely in the enormous closet. "I thought Orlando was filled with northerners."

"We're a mixture of all kinds of people, like most areas of the state. Why?"

"You have a Southern accent." She carried her travel kit to the bathroom countertop which boasted two double sinks, but she didn't unpack her toothbrush and makeup. She was too busy fantasizing about the gargantuan whirlpool tub that was more than big enough for two. "It's a good thing I know how to swim."

When he didn't respond, she drew her gaze from that inviting tub to his face. Totally unprepared for the desire radiating from his gaze, she was stunned by the potency of his interest. Her pulse accelerated until heat flushed her skin. If he could arouse her with just a look, what would happen if he touched her again? Or gave her a kiss more deep than a brushing of lips?

"I was hoping you'd need a lifeguard." His eyes flared with heat.

"I still hold the high school state record for the hundred meter backstroke." However, it was breaststroke she was thinking about and not the kind accomplished in a swimming competition. "Someone to wash my back might be…nice."

"I'm right down that hall." He pointed, then redirected her gaze to a nightstand beside the bed. "See the intercom? Just call and I'll be here."

She stared at him wondering how he'd suddenly

notched up the sexual energy with no more than a searing look. Usually she was immune to such things. In fact, she preferred to be friends before moving on to a more intimate relationship. Amanda was simply not the kind of woman to jump into bed with a hot guy—and yet, for some reason, Bolt seemed to bring out her impulsive and naughty side.

But it wasn't right to lead him on. "I was kidding about washing my back."

"I wasn't." His tone turned serious. His gaze flickered with an emotion she couldn't read, reminding her that she'd only met him last night.

She barely knew him, and yet she sensed he was holding back something important. Despite his interest, despite his flirtatious attitude, it was almost as if he wanted to warn her...but about what?

An odd shiver careened down her back and she touched the gun at her shoulder holster for reassurance. She wasn't worried about Bolt forcing her to do anything she didn't want to do. The Shey Group didn't hire men who would attack a woman. The organization had a reputation for hiring only the very best of the best, at least according to the FBI director's e-mail.

And yet...all her instincts were on high alert. For one thing, her own reactions to this man kept surprising her. Sure she found Bolt interesting, fascinating and exciting, but that still didn't explain her almost overwhelming desire to tease him. Usually Amanda was perfectly content to go slowly. To think before she spoke. She was not a spontaneous person. Yet she wouldn't know it from some of the flirting she'd been doing.

Bolt had every right to think she might use that intercom to call him for a little nighttime action between the sheets. But she wouldn't call him, of course. Safe, practical, steady Amanda didn't do one-night stands. She didn't have flings. She didn't even think about sex that often. Although she had her share of offers, since Donna's death, she hadn't been on so much as a date.

And before Donna had died, she'd been busy raising her sister and working on her career. Amanda had never had the luxury of considering her own feelings first. Since her parents' deaths she'd always had to think how her actions might affect her sister. While that was no longer the case, her personality had been set such a long time ago that she didn't expect to change.

Perhaps her body was sex starved, but Amanda had to be emotionally involved to be turned on. So what was going on between her and Bolt? Amanda wasn't sure she believed in lust at first sight, never mind love at first sight. But she couldn't deny that the two of them had definitely clicked.

But surely the connection wasn't all sensory. She couldn't deny she liked looking at him and enjoyed his intense blue eyes, his George Clooney jaw, his wrap-me-up-and-take-me-home smile. But was his overwhelming physical impact enough to make her change the behavior of a lifetime? She certainly didn't think so.

And yet…she couldn't deny her pummeling heart. Or her shallow breaths. Or the damp heat pooling between her thighs.

"WOULD YOU LIKE TO SEE the surveillance room?" Bolt offered.

As experienced as he was around women, Amanda confused him. One moment she was all sass and giving him come-and-take-me glances, the next she was trying to convince him her suggestive comments were made in jest.

So was she fighting a real attraction to him? Or was something else at work? The Shey Group knew too little about the supposed paranormal effects of the perfume bottle for him to guess if it could have anything to do with her contradictory behavior. But the idea that lingering aftereffects from exposure to Hathaway and the perfume bottle last night could now cause her to do things she wouldn't normally do creeped him out.

He had enough pride that he wanted a woman to like him for himself. Anything else seemed dishonest and wrong. So as much as he would have liked to continue flirting with the very delectable Miss Amanda Lane, relief filled him when she wanted to see the surveillance equipment.

The Shey Group had removed all the regular furnishings from the second room on the main wing. Along the room's far wall, a bank of monitors revealed various angles inside Hathaway's penthouse. Microphones allowed them to hear conversations while tape machines, automatically activated by sound, recorded every word.

Bolt watched Amanda take in the setup, her gaze widening. "Do we have a warrant?"

So she'd either heard or suspected that the Shey Group sometimes bent the rules. Testing her knowledge, he said, "I'll pretend you didn't ask that question."

"We're breaking the law." She frowned. "I'm not sure if I can—"

"We have a warrant," he lied, ready to produce a fake document if necessary.

Bolt didn't like lying to his partner, but she was an FBI Agent, and if by chance things went wrong, he wanted her to be able to truthfully deny all responsibility for unlawful procedures—not that Logan Kincaid would ever allow such circumstances to come to light. Too many federal judges, never mind congressmen and women, owed him favors. However, since the lie protected Amanda, he could live with himself.

"Nice." She peered at the monitors that showed Hathaway's cook in the kitchen preparing a meal. A maid vacuumed the living area and a gardener watered indoor plants and replaced wilted flowers that floated in a water-filled urn. "You don't have anything in the bedroom and master bath?"

"When the cook took a day off, our replacement 'cook' couldn't get in there or into the home office, either."

"Are the phones tapped?" she asked.

He shook his head. "Hathaway's careful. He'd got an encryption program most of the free world would envy."

"If he's that careful, why hasn't he found your electronic bugs?"

"He will. It's only a matter of time."

She frowned at him, thinking through the implications. "But once Hathaway learns we're watching him, he'll be more careful and more difficult to catch."

"That's why we need to find a way to infiltrate his organization real soon. How're your typing skills?"

"Hunt and peck. Why?"

"We could arrange for Hathaway's executive assistant to come down with strep throat. Then we'd give you a résumé he can't resist."

"And when he finds out that I can't type?"

"Not a problem. I'll install software that's voice activated. You'll be a pro inside ten minutes."

"And then?"

"We wait for Hathaway to find the electronic bugs. Bugs that lead him to believe his security team has a leak. You suggest that he hire someone new. Me."

"I thought he only hires women."

"Women form his inner circle. But he'll hire a man when necessary. I'm not letting you go in there alone."

"Why not?" Her eyes searched his and he realized she must have picked up additional tension from him. He hadn't changed his voice or expression or posture, but nevertheless her question revealed her suspicion that he hadn't told her everything.

He kept his answer vague and casual. "You might need backup close by."

She opened her mouth to say more but the front doors of Hathaway's penthouse opened and a crowd of well-dressed, tall and thin women barged into the swank living area, Hathaway in their midst. "Do we know who these women are?"

Leaning forward, Bolt turned up the sound. "None of them is a top executive. From their looks, I suspect they are models."

"Did you notice the cook, maid and gardener were all gorgeous, too?" she asked, sounding wary of a man who surrounded himself with only extraordinarily good-looking people. She stared hard at the monitor as if trying to find a flaw in one of them.

"Hathaway." A willowy brunette trailed a finger down his arm. Her bright scarlet nail scraped from his open collar to his shirt's top button. "You promised me some fun."

"And you shall have it, darling."

Her collagen lips pouted. "Didn't anyone ever tell you that three is a crowd and five—"

"Is an orgy." Another woman leaned over and nuzzled the brunette's ear and giggled.

Amanda goggled and swallowed hard. She licked her bottom lip, her pink tongue sexy as hell.

"I suppose if I can't have you all to myself I can share," the brunette said.

"That's the spirit." Hathaway broke out a bottle of wine and poured four glasses, one for each woman.

Clearly mesmerized, Amanda barely moved and Bolt wondered once again about how the bottle worked and if she could be affected over a monitor.

"We need music," the blonde suggested.

"Dim the lights," said a redhead whose words made her sound modest, but who had already pulled off her top. Her silicone breasts swung free to reveal both nipples pierced with gold-hooped rings.

"They're so casual," Amanda commented, her voice tight as she studied the women.

"Something wrong?" Bolt asked, concerned that if watching this scene upset her, she might not be the right person for the job, after all. From his research, he'd learned that Hathaway had an enormous appetite for the ladies.

"I just can't imagine my sister…as one of those women." Amanda's gaze never left the screen and she swayed on her feet.

Bolt understood. She was reluctant to accept the idea that her sister could have participated in such shocking behavior, and been killed by Hathaway. While he sympathized, he needed to know, before they inserted her into Hathaway's operation, that she could handle this scene. "If watching upsets you, then perhaps you should leave."

"I'm not going anywhere." She spoke with determination but as if her knees had buckled, she plopped into a chair, her eyes focused on the screens. "We need to know what's going on."

All of the woman were in various states of undress.

And though they'd dimmed the lighting, many details were clear. Between sips of wine, Hathaway let the women takes turns caressing, kissing, stroking and undressing him. For such a round-faced man, he had more muscles than Bolt would have guessed and he made a mental note to check the client lists of New York's more exclusive fitness clubs to see if he worked out. Before he was done investigating, he would know the man's routine as well as his sexual preferences.

Amanda leaned forward and her hands clenched the arms of her chair. "Do these women seem…normal to you?"

"What do you mean?" Did she see something paranormal that he didn't?

"Zoom in on their eyes, please. I'd like to determine if he's drugged the women before we assume he has special paranormal abilities. I want to see if their pupils are regular size."

He did as she asked, waiting for the right moment to stop the video stream, then zooming in. "Their irises look dilated to me."

"Could he have drugged the wine?" she asked. "Or is this a side effect from the bottle's unusual properties?"

Adjusting the camera, he zoomed in on Hathaway. The agent's expression was like a sultan enjoying his harem. Bolt could only imagine what watching this scene was doing to Amanda as she thought about her sister taking the place of one of those women. If Hathaway had been using one of Bolt's sisters in such a fashion, he would have been hard put to refrain from charging over there, shoving his fist down the pervert's throat and ripping out his heart.

He forced himself to analyze. "Hathaway's eyes appear normal." Bolt didn't think the man's behavior made him seem drugged, either, or at least not as far gone as the women. "And he drank the wine out of the same carafe."

Amanda glared at the screen, her expression fierce. "He's larger and carries more body weight. Maybe a drug wouldn't affect him so much. Or maybe, earlier, he put a substance in the bottom of each glass, but not his. Or maybe the drug only affects women."

Or maybe the paranormal effects of the perfume bottle had stimulated the women and caused their inhibitions to lower and their lusts to increase. "Or maybe," Bolt suggested, "they are turned on naturally. Eyes do dilate when a person's aroused."

"I suppose…" But Amanda didn't sound convinced. "I wish we could get a sample of that wine for analysis."

"The cook isn't due for another day off until next week."

"What about the maid?" Amanda crossed and uncrossed her legs, fidgeting in her seat as if she couldn't get comfortable.

"Maria Gonzalez never takes a day off. She's from the poorest section of Mexico City and needs every cent to send back home."

Amanda's fingers clutched the arms of her chair. The cords in her graceful neck tightened, and her chin was so high and her spine so ramrod straight she clearly had to force herself to sit still. The women were all naked now, as was Hathaway, their clothes strewn about the room like confetti.

"The cook is heading toward the living room," Amanda's tone was hushed in anticipation. "I can't imagine what she's going to think."

Bolt had no idea if the cook would run away screaming, phone the police, or scamper back into the kitchen and pretend she hadn't seen the writhing, squirming bodies, the eager mouths and seeking hands that overflowed the couch and sprawled onto the carpets.

The cook's steps were quick. When she set down a tray of cheese snacks and began to remove her shirt, Amanda gasped.

"She's joining them. This is freakin' unbelievable. It's like a scene out of Dante's *Inferno*."

Amanda didn't sound so much disgusted as baffled and amazed that paranormal perfume bottles really did exist. He drew her attention from the main action. "Look at the maid on the third monitor."

"Sheesh," Amanda said, shaking her head. "The maid's so eager to join the fray, she's not even waiting to enter the room before she strips." Her eyebrows arched and she rubbed her fingers over her lips. "Either Hathaway has more natural charisma than any man alive or…"

"Or?"

"He must be using something like hypnosis to attract so many women, to convince them to…to…boink like bunnies…"

Bolt tried to restrain a chuckle at her description. "We

haven't eliminated all the natural explanations. Maybe he's paying them. We'll investigate his bank accounts as well as those of the ladies he's with once we find out their names."

"And how will you do that?"

"We have face recognition software. The program compiles the information on every person the camera picks up. We're testing the software for the CIA."

Amanda shook her head, but her voice dropped to a husky tone. "I'm willing to bet you don't find anything. A man like Hathaway doesn't have to pay for sex. And those women look too eager. They aren't faking it. They're hot for him, just like my sister was. And none of it makes sense unless..."

"Unless?"

She slapped her palm on the table in obvious frustration. "I might buy into the notion that these women are there for good sex and only good sex...except—"

"Except?" he prodded.

She lowered her tone to a whisper. "You'll think I'm insane."

"Try me." He leaned forward, not wanting to miss a word. Her intensity fascinated him. Her reaction to the monitors intrigued him.

"Last night, I tried to meet Hathaway, but I never got close to him."

"So?"

"We exchanged a look."

"A look?"

"It was almost like a whip snapping through the air.

A command. A soundless…compulsion. I believe he used that paranormal power on me—just like he's now using it on these women."

Bolt refrained from releasing a long, low whistle. Was she even now sensing the paranormal effect of the bottle, an effect that enhanced Hathaway's attraction to women?

"A compulsion to do what?" he asked, unwilling to lead her or make a suggestion to sidetrack her.

"I'm not sure."

"Try to tell me."

"It was unlike anything I've ever known." Amanda shivered, crossed her arms across her chest and rubbed her palms on her arms. "All right, tell me I'm insane, and we'll just pretend we didn't have this conversation."

He tried to lighten the moment. "Perhaps, your sister is trying to tell you something from the grave."

"Don't patronize me," she snapped at him and her stormy eyes flashed with irritation. "I damn sure don't believe in ghosts."

He held up his hands, palms facing her. "Hey, I was out of line. I apologize."

"Apology accepted," she said without hesitation, revealing that she didn't hold grudges. Unclasping her hands from her arms, she drew her knees to her chest and rested her chin on her knees. "I'm not given to flights of fancy."

"Flights of fancy?"

"I don't have a vivid imagination. I rarely remember my dreams. I prefer to believe what my senses tell me. That's why I didn't want to bring up my feeling. But when Hathaway and I locked gazes, something connected us. Something evil and lurid." She shuddered and glanced at the naked, writhing bodies on the screen, then looked away. "And do you know what is really sick?"

"Hathaway?"

"Besides Hathaway."

"What?"

"I don't like pornography. Give me a good romance with lots of emotion and lovemaking where people care about one another and I'm a happy camper."

"But?"

She raised her tormented gaze to him. And then she blinked and the light caught her gaze at a different angle. Her pupils had dilated, her nostrils flared slightly. She was clasping her knees to her chest to prevent him from seeing her trembling.

He'd thought she was shivering because she was tense and upset from watching the orgy. But she wasn't. She was shaking with desire. Hiding her very erect nipples.

"I don't understand it. But I swear to you, if I was in that room with Hathaway right now, I might not be able to resist joining in."

"What?"

"That's right. You heard me." She dropped her head, as if in shame, then again raised her chin, eyes ferocious, voice tortured with anger and desire. "I want to screw a man I don't even know, a man with whom I've never exchanged a word. The man who likely killed my sister. So tell me. Bolt—" her voice broke in desperation "—how in hell am I going to resist him?"

4

OH…MY…GOD.

Amanda didn't understand why watching an orgy had her so turned on that she was shaking with need. She never lost control. Through her entire conversation with Bolt, she'd tried to remain professionally detached, and yet she couldn't resist the monumental forces building up pressure inside her body. Her pulse raced and skidded, her temperature rose. Her skin sizzled. And while her brain was disgusted and repelled by Hathaway, her body was on fire.

"I'm here for you," Bolt assured her, his eyes full of questions.

"I don't understand what's happening," she whispered through her need, a need so great that she wanted to rip off her clothes and tackle Bolt like some kind of love-starved maniac. What was wrong with her? She didn't do unbridled passion. Yet she had to grip the chair's armrests to keep her hands from ripping his shirt open—and all because she'd watched Hathaway with those models.

Bolt gestured to the monitor. "Porn is a profitable business, there's no shame in reacting—"

She shook her head; certain other forces were in play. "Hathaway is likely responsible for Donna's murder," she panted, unable to hold back the shiver of desire coursing through her, "yet my hormones are going wild."

He placed reassuring hands on her shoulders. "Just try to—"

At his touch, she was on her feet and flinging herself into his arms before she understood what she'd done. Her sudden rush was as instinctual as stumbling, then fighting for balance. Her sole thought was that she must touch and be touched. She needed the contact of his flesh against hers, the scent of him in her lungs, the heat of him warming her.

As his arms closed around her and his mouth slanted over hers, all sane thinking ceased. This kiss was no mere brushing of the lips. If this kiss had been a hurricane it would have been a class five. If this kiss had been a prize, it would have been the Nobel. If this kiss had been a rocket, it would have shot out of the solar system, straight to a galaxy far, far away.

Clutching his shoulders to draw him even closer, his clean male scent spurred her on. Boldly, brazenly, she kissed him, dazzled by the taste of sizzling brawn peppered with torrid heat. Her lips burned for him and after one long, bone-melting kiss, she was hot enough to go up in flames.

Never before had her lips swelled with passion. Every lick, nip and nibble kicked her other senses into overdrive. His breath rasped and merged with the roaring of blood in her ears. She ripped at his shirt with tingling hands desperate to remove the material separating their flesh. Their kiss heated, then erupted into a hard-boiled hysteria she'd never known.

Her clumsy fingers fumbled with his shirt. And then she was torn between wanting to touch his muscular shoulders, rugged back and solid ribs, or to explore his powerful chest dusted with crisp curls of fine black hair, or just go for broke and unzip his slacks.

She went for broke. The need to have all of him bared couldn't wait. In no mood for finesse, for teasing, for foreplay, she wanted him now. She wanted him hard and fast. She wanted him inside her without another moment's delay.

Breathless and panting, she fumbled, her entire body shaking with her fervor. She was burning up for him, like a fever was racing through her blood, a fever that only he could assuage.

Their prolonged kiss slowed the progress of her hands, but she couldn't give up his wonderful mouth—not even to rip off his clothes. As their tongues danced, he in turn managed to remove her shirt and bra. Her breasts sprang free, her nipples already swollen and ripe and oh-so-ready to press against his bare chest.

But keeping them apart, his hands skimmed up her waist, cupping her, his thumbs flicking over her sensitive nipples and shooting heat straight between her thighs. Moisture, slick and thick, readied her sex. She was certain she would burst the moment he entered her, but she had yet to remove his slacks.

Between his magic hands and clever tongue, she couldn't seem to direct her hands. Moaning with the frustration of wanting him that instant, she finally wrenched her mouth free.

"I can't wait," she muttered, tugging at his belt, finally unsnapping his slacks and shoving trousers and boxers to the floor in one smooth thrust. "I must have you. Now."

She closed her fingers over his smooth, hard sex, pleased that he was so ready for her. With her mouth on his, she enjoyed the sensation of his pulsing male flesh in her hand. As she swirled her tongue over his and explored the soft texture of his lips, she was gratified when his balls coiled tightly at her exploratory touch.

She ached to venture further, but he placed his hands on her waist and lifted her until she was forced to release him. Dizzy, breathless, slightly confused, she found herself standing before him on a chair.

With a wicked gleam in his eyes, he made swift work of removing the rest of her clothes. With her breasts in his face, he needed no urging to take a nipple into his mouth. As sweet-spicy sensations washed over her, she couldn't hold back a sob of pleasure.

"Oh. Don't stop." She cradled his head, drawing his mouth closer.

His wonderfully skilled tongue teased and tugged her areolae with erotic strokes. His fingers urged her to part her thighs, and when his hand slid into home, his thumb centering on where all her nerves were most sensitive, she cried out and gyrated her hips.

His teeth clamped down on her nipple, restraining her, holding her exactly where he wanted. Overwhelmed by the sensations of his flickering fingers and taunting mouth, the tension inside her tummy knotted, swelled, then spiraled, until she had to clench his shoulders just to stay upright.

"Oh…my."

"Tell me what you'd like," he demanded without releasing her nipple.

"Everything."

"You're sure?" He flicked her clit.

She gulped as heat poured through her. "Anything."

"Okay."

"Just don't stop…doing…what you're doing."

He laughed low and deep, his breath a sexy whoosh against her flesh. "No problem."

Contradicting his words, he released her nipple and air soothed over the wet pouty skin. But then he took the other one into his mouth, and she would have sighed with the pleasure, except the sensation was too strong for sighs. In fact, she was having a hell of a lot of trouble holding back a scream of *yes, yes, yes.*

Bursting, burning, she was so ready to have him inside her. "I need you in me."

"Can't."

"What!" She was going to lose it. She was shaking with need. Trembling. So tight, so ready.

"Condoms are…in the…bedroom."

She groaned. No way could she walk that far. She doubted she could take a step before her knees buckled.

"It's okay." His fingers moved back and forth inside her slickness, the marvelous friction stretching her.

"Ah. Oh-oh." She couldn't draw enough air. Her lungs burned. The pleasure from his tongue, his fingers, his thumb created hot sparks that caught. One moment she was tense and blistering and on edge. The next, she went up in flames.

Like a wildfire that burned out of control, she blazed with the scalding heat. She gasped with the exquisite burning that seemed to go on and on and on. And when she finally came back to herself, she was in his arms and he was carrying her to the bedroom.

With her limbs relaxed, her mind still fuzzy, she was perfectly willing to let him take control. Thinking about the reason for her impulsive lovemaking was simply too much trouble. Especially after such a mind-blowing orgasm.

She'd had orgasms before. But never one like that—not even from her vibrator. Wow. On the Richter scale, the one he'd just given her would be a ten. She'd had no idea that she could feel this good with a man, never mind one she barely knew.

Snuggling against his chest, his strong arms easily carrying her, she'd never felt so feminine. Usually the taking-off-her-clothes process was embarrassingly awkward. She'd preferred the lights down low. She'd been self-conscious. But not with Bolt. The passion had burst upon her so fast and hard, she hadn't once thought about the extra weight on her hips, or if her thighs were tight, or if…well, it didn't matter now. He'd seen her naked and from the look of fervor on his face, he liked what he'd seen.

Leaning her head back on his arm, she gazed at him, enjoying the sparkle in his expression, the amused lips, the determined jut of his jaw and the playful glow of his eyes. "We are going to make love again, right?"

"We need to talk."

"Talk?" Her brow furrowed. "I don't want to talk." She reached up and placed the tip of her finger on his mouth. "I can think of much better things for you to do with those lips."

"You may change your mind," he warned.

But she wouldn't. Nothing he said was going to convince her that she didn't want another kiss.

BOLT'S EVERY MALE chromosome ached to tell her that he would make love to her all night, all day and into next week if that was what she wanted. Nibbling on her delicious mouth and her delectable breasts had only been the appetizer. His body was hungrily demanding a ten-course feast, and he wanted to devour every savory inch of her.

And yet, his conscience wouldn't let him. When he hadn't believed in the perfume bottle's paranormal powers, it was fine to make love to her if she wanted him to. But after witnessing her reaction to Hathaway and his "party," Bolt could no longer deny that Amanda was influenced by a power he couldn't explain.

He'd read her dossier, and her past had revealed that Amanda wasn't the kind of woman to take a lover lightly. She'd had only two relationships, one during her last two years of college, the other a few years ago. In both cases, she'd known the men for a long time before she'd become involved.

And knowing what he did about Amanda, knowing what Kincaid had told him about the perfume bottle, he now believed they needed to talk about the perfume bottle's effect before he went further. Taking her away from the monitor and Hathaway had been the first step. Already he could see the haze clearing from her gaze and the questions beginning to arise.

He gritted his teeth and attempted to ignore his aching balls, his pounding lust, his need to sheathe his sex inside her. Amanda was no longer a woman in a file. She was his partner and he wanted her respect. And he couldn't earn that if he took advantage of her.

Gently he placed her on his bed and pulled a sheet over her so he wouldn't be distracted by all her tempting flesh. He had to say this right. Combing his fingers through his hair, he considered where to begin, but with her dark hair fanning the pillow and her curious eyes on him, he was having difficulty collecting his thoughts.

"What I'm about to tell you is going to sound farfetched at best."

She nodded and he appreciated her patience. He took a seat beside her, propped a pillow behind his back and flipped the sheet over his erection, hoping out of site would equate to out of mind. Not likely after what they'd so recently shared, but he wanted her full attention on his words.

She rolled onto her side, and elbow crooked, propped

her head on her palm. Her other hand, she rested lightly on his knee. "I'm listening."

"I believe that somehow the paranormal effects of the perfume bottle Hathaway stole turned you on."

She snorted. "Now, there's a leap in logic, especially since I've never seen the bottle, let alone touched it."

"We don't know how the paranormal effects work. Maybe the bottle emits a scent into the air and you breathed it in."

"The only time I've been near Hathaway was during that party last night. You think I breathed in an aphrodisiac, and it didn't activate in my system until now?"

"Suppose the drug activates when a key word is spoken," he suggested. "Maybe Hathaway said something on the monitor that made you respond."

She eyed him warily. "Is such a thing possible?"

He shrugged in frustration. "I don't know. Our mission is to reclaim the bottle for its rightful owner, not necessarily figure out how it works. You never so much as shook Hathaway's hand last night, right?"

"Correct." She hesitated, shivered, then wrapped the sheet tighter around her. "But he looked at me oddly."

He tried not to frown. "You mentioned that before. Can you explain it a little better?"

"It's difficult to describe. But even at the time, I noticed that I couldn't look away. As if his drilling stare compelled me to…to…"

"To what?"

"I don't know. It just felt weird. Then I met you and I forgot about him." She swallowed hard, but bravely held his gaze. Bolt realized that if he ever married, he'd want a partner as courageous as Amanda. "Do you believe I was immediately attracted to you at the party due to something Hathaway did?"

"It's possible." He suspected that admitting such private thoughts was extremely difficult for her. Yet, she did so in such a straightforward and honest manner that his compassion soared and made his determination to protect her harden.

She lowered her tone but her words were clear. "And then when I practically attacked you just now...that's not exactly characteristic behavior for me." Her fist tightened in the sheet. "I was drowning in lust. Out of control. I could think of nothing but having you. Even now the residual effects may still be in my system. I may not be thinking clearly. I'm sorry."

"For what?"

Her eyes flickered with pain before she looked away and gestured to his groin, where he remained at half-mast. "Obviously you didn't want to go through with—"

"Nothing could be further from the truth." How could she think he didn't want her? Even now, his blood still simmered and he ached with the lack of release. After what she admitted, he could do no less than the same. "I wanted you. I still do. But I wouldn't take advantage of a woman who'd drunk too much alcohol. And whatever affected you was out of your control. I thought we should be on the same page before...continuing."

"I see."

"No, I don't think you do." She needed to hear it all,

his every hypothesis and ugly suspicion because if they were going to keep on working together she would do so with her eyes wide-open and every theory at her disposal. "If you continue as my partner, it's likely that Hathaway will repeatedly trigger the same reaction from you. This is going to sound crazy…but I'm prepared to keep you satisfied so that you won't fall under his complete influence."

Her eyes went wide and her face flushed. He didn't believe she was blushing from embarrassment. On the contrary, she seemed turned on by the idea. But was her reaction due to a genuine attraction to Bolt? Or due to the effect of the damn bottle? He wished he knew.

"So you're volunteering to keep me sexually satisfied?" Her tone rose into an almost hysterical giggle.

"It may be necessary." He shrugged. "If you back out now, I'll understand."

"Why didn't you tell me everything right from the beginning?" she demanded, her eyes flashing with heat.

"Because I didn't really think this could happen. And even if I'd told you, I didn't think you'd believe me anyway."

"And what changed your mind?"

Knowing his words might frighten her, he nevertheless told her the truth as he saw it. "You went from a regular conversation to hot so fast that the change seemed…uncontrollable."

She bit her bottom lip, rolled to her back and stared at the ceiling. "If I back out, what would you do?"

At the question, disappointment shot through him. "I'd find someone else. But you were our first choice."

"Because of my sister?"

"And because of your FBI training."

She spoke slowly. "I don't know what to say. I want to nail Hathaway for Donna. I want to clear her name. And if he's manipulating other women...I'd like to stop him, too." She closed her eyes for a moment, then opened them. "Suppose he sets me off when you aren't around?"

"That won't happen." He couldn't keep the growl from his tone.

"And you're ready to...to..."

"Keep you so damn satisfied that you aren't going to want anyone but me."

AMANDA WANTED TO SAY yes to Bolt's plan, but was she thinking clearly, or was the sexual haze of pleasure Bolt had created clouding her judgment? Or was the damn bottle responsible for her yearning to toss all caution aside and allow Bolt to take care of her every sexual need?

He certainly was capable of doing so. She had no doubts about that after her wondrous orgasm.

But the idea of being out of control unnerved her. Amanda didn't ever drink more than a glass of wine. She didn't do drugs. The notion of the bottle messing with her mind scared her on several levels. If she couldn't trust her own feelings, then she'd have to rely on Bolt—a man she'd known for barely twenty-four hours. He was asking for a lot of her trust, perhaps more than she had to give.

Although she was well aware of the Shey Group's reputation, Hathaway was a dangerous man. He'd proven that by getting away with murder. And they weren't dealing with normal criminal activities. If the bottle affected her mind, they had no idea what Hathaway might influence her to do.

And yet, Amanda recalled the last time Donna's enthusiastic voice had zinged through the telephone lines. She still remembered every word they'd exchanged and her own thoughts at the time that now left her with so much guilt.

Donna had sounded so vibrant. "Sis, Hathaway's the best boss I've ever had."

"Yeah, right," Amanda had snorted then sipped her coffee, pleased to hear her sister's sarcasm rather than more bitterness over her recent divorce.

Ever since Donna's cheating, no-good ex had left her, Amanda's younger sister had sworn off men for good. So her phone call revealing a new attitude had come as a welcome surprise.

Perhaps Donna's sudden job change had done her good after all, at least improving her sense of humor. Her sister hadn't been thinking clearly for months, so Amanda had feared she'd taken the new job based on the wrong reasons. Last year, after Donna had successfully proven the viability of her patent, she could have written her own ticket in the defense industry. McDonald Douglas had offered her stock perks and a golden parachute to woo her to their company. But when Donna's husband had left their marriage for a stage starlet, Donna had careened into a one-eighty-degree career change.

Amanda had never understood her sister's insistence on leaving a job where she was highly paid and respected to one where she'd be treated like a piece of meat. Modeling was not known to help a woman's self-esteem. Why a woman with a genius IQ would want to model for Hathaway Balkmandy was beyond Amanda. But high intelligence didn't necessarily go hand-in-hand with good judgment and Donna had always been flighty, requiring Amanda to be the steady, practical sister ever since their parents had died.

After months of talking doom and gloom, Donna was brightening up the phone lines with her enthusiasm. "My boss Hathaway is so rich he's promising to fly me to Paris for the spring shows on a private jet."

Amanda laughed. "Glad to see you're over Ryan."

"Ryan? Who's Ryan?"

"That's the spirit."

Amanda had been head cheerleader as well as both mom and dad to her sister for well over a decade. While her brilliant sister had skipped two years of high school, then went on to earn her Ph.D. in record time, Amanda had had no choice but to grow up fast. Judging by the mistakes her sister had made, as a surrogate parent, Amanda hadn't done such a great job.

Amanda wasn't sure where she'd gone wrong. Perhaps she'd been too overprotective. But what twenty-two-year-old was prepared to parent a rebellious sixteen-year-old?

"There's only one problem," Donna chattered on.

"You snagged a nail and need another manicure?" Amanda teased.

"Very funny. Modeling is hard work, you know."

"Yeah, I'm sure it's very taxing on your brain," Amanda muttered, then could have bitten her tongue for speaking so freely. She'd put herself through college on the life insurance her parents had left, then worked double shifts to put Donna through, too. And she couldn't hide her concern. But who was Amanda to say that her sister wouldn't be happier peddling her good looks than using her brain?

She sighed. She just wanted her sister to be happy. Odd, how Donna had gotten the brains and the good looks, yet of the two women, Amanda was much happier. Perhaps she didn't expect as much. She didn't seem to have Donna's highs and lows, living in the saner middle ground. Down to earth and practical, she was the provider, the one who everyone depended on in a crisis.

Amanda had done her best and thrown her heart into parenting her sister, but it had been a rocky road at best. Yet despite her single-minded endeavor to raise her sister in a practical and levelheaded manner, Amanda's efforts hadn't prevented Donna from piercing her tongue, her navel and probably several other areas that Amanda would rather not know about. But Amanda had thought her worst mistake, by far, had been urging Donna to marry Ryan. Amanda had believed marriage would settle her sister. And in truth, she'd looked forward to sharing the responsibility and expense of her sister, who never seemed to earn enough money to support her expensive taste in clothes.

"So what's the problem?" she asked her sister, expecting another one-liner.

"Hathaway's so exciting that every woman who comes near him wants him as much as I do."

"What?" Amanda almost spit her coffee onto her desk. "You aren't serious, are you?"

"Of course I'm serious. The man is so cute—"

"Please." Amanda's concerned-sister radar went into overdrive. "I thought you'd sworn off men."

"I did. But Hathaway is amazing, and I'm not talking about his talent for picking models, or his 5th Avenue penthouse, or his stretch limo."

"Then what are you talking about?"

"The man has charisma with a capital C."

"So does Quentin Tarantino. That doesn't mean I'd date him."

"Hathaway may like to party, but he's a businessman, first and foremost."

Amanda barely restrained another snort. Hathaway might be wealthy but she thought of him in the same light as Larry Flynt and Hugh Hefner, certainly not suitable husband material. "Let me get this straight. You're attracted to him?"

"Along with every other woman in N.Y."

Amanda wanted to shout at her sister to take the next train out of Manhattan. Every muscle in her tensed as she tried to remember that Donna was now a grown woman and had to be allowed to make her own mistakes. But those mistakes always had consequences and somehow it always remained Amanda's task to come barreling to the rescue.

She attempted to keep her temper under control. Good men weren't easy to find—and N.Y.C. was notoriously hard on single women.

Besides, her sister had to be on an emotional roller coaster after her divorce, surely not thinking clearly. However, she might be brought to see reason with logic. Amanda strummed her fingers on her desk. "If Hathaway doesn't think you're special enough to ditch those other women for, then he has no taste. So why would you want him?"

"Because…he's irresistible."

Amanda should have hung up the phone, taken the next train into the city and dragged her sister out of Hathaway's clutches. Instead Amanda had hoped Donna was going through a phase. Besides, at the time, she'd been trying to track down the "Soul of God," an extremist group reputed to be importing a truckload of C-4 into Newark airport. Unfortunately her intelligence had never panned out.

And she'd never spoken to Donna again. Amanda still felt guilty for failing to stop her sister from working for Hathaway. She should have put aside her FBI work, given it to an associate and checked out the agent's credentials, his reputation with women. If she had, she might have saved Donna's life.

Amanda would go to her own grave wishing she'd done something to help her sister. But she hadn't, and she'd lost her forever.

She wasn't the kind of woman who usually involved herself in dangerous missions. Her forte was research, putting together hints of intel from a variety of sources to obtain the big picture. But she couldn't banish the image of Donna's body in a Dumpster. And to clear her sister's name and help put away the man who'd murdered her, Amanda had to take a few risks. If she had to lose a little control and ended up making passionate love to sexy Bolt Tanner, well, that was the price she'd pay to do what must be done. In truth, even if Amanda hadn't found Bolt so attractive and considerate, she wouldn't have decided differently. The fact that she would enjoy the particular decision was something she didn't want to think about right now, especially while Bolt was waiting so patiently for her answer.

However, before she gave him a reply, she wanted to know more about Bolt. Turning back onto her side, she kept her tone level, ignoring that both of them were naked beneath the sheet. "Why did you take this mission?"

"Working for the Shey Group is what I do."

"Did you know beforehand that you might be required to…that I might need…" She felt like an idiot for not being able to say she might need a stud service. But that made what he'd just done for her sound demeaning.

He grinned, asking her question for her. "Did I know that you might need my help remaining sexually satisfied to avoid the effects of a perfume bottle? Yes, I suspected. But I wasn't certain."

"Suppose you'd found me unattractive?" She watched him closely, expecting him to prevaricate.

But he responded simply. "Then I would have suggested another man take the job."

"The decision was that easy for you?"

He ticked off points on his fingers. "One, I like what I do. Two, I'm well paid. And three, I was attracted to you from the moment I saw you. So the decision was pretty much a no-brainer."

Curious that his thinking process was so straightforward, without all the ifs, ands and buts that she normally went through before deciding anything of major importance, she watched to see if the mention of emotions would cause him to back off or squirm. "But what if your feelings for me grew?"

He didn't so much as blink. "That would be another plus, don't you think?"

She laughed. "Are you always such an optimist?"

"What's not to be optimistic about when I have a naked, beautiful woman in my bed?"

He had a point. But he obviously looked at the situation very differently than she did. He wasn't the one whose mind was being messed with by a bottle. He wasn't the one who didn't know if he could trust his own thoughts and feelings. And he wasn't the one whose sister had died.

"Didn't you enjoy yourself back there?" He gestured to the room where he'd satisfied her wild craving.

"You know I did."

"So would making love be any different now?"

"Of course." She eyed him with a frown. "I had no idea what was happening until you explained. But if I agree, I'll be doing so with full knowledge."

He shook his head. "I'm not sure I understand what—"

"Sure you do. That's why you explained to me exactly what was happening. So it would be my choice. Either I walk away, or I stay and take the risk of losing all control over myself and my actions."

"And?"

"Deciding is difficult when I don't know if the damn bottle is still affecting my mind or my emotions right now."

"So you want me to take you home?"

She liked that he didn't try to talk her into anything. His willingness to accept her decision put a final stamp on her resolution to stay and become his partner. "Actually I'm going through with the plan."

"You're sure?"

"Very."

She thought he would take her into his arms, seal their partnership with a hug or a kiss. But instead he locked his hands behind his head and settled against his pillows and the headboard. "We need to create a cover for you."

His change of subject was actually a relief. Her earlier ardor had cooled. Not that she didn't still find him attractive. She did. But she could think more clearly now, and she wanted to know more about Bolt and their mission.

"Hathaway saw me at his party but we never spoke. I'm sure he has no idea that I'm Donna's sister."

"Good. The Shey Group can create a cover for you

in a few hours. You should keep the name Amanda, so you respond naturally, but we'll change your last name. After we give Hathaway's current executive assistant strep throat, since we want you to apply for her job, we'll create a suitable background."

"He might remember me from the party."

"You can say you'd inveigled an invite from a friend in hopes of landing a job."

"Seems simple enough."

"Let's hope so." Bolt picked up the phone, all business. "I'll order the credentials you'll require and set the rest in motion."

5

DURING THE PAST FEW DAYS, Amanda had stayed out of the surveillance room and had suffered from no further bouts of unexplainable lust. She'd let Bolt monitor Hathaway while she'd prepared to go undercover. Despite her FBI training, she'd never been in the field.

Memorizing her new background wasn't too difficult. The Shey Group had done a marvelous job of creating a past similar to her own. Since her cover didn't require anything deep, she remained the same age, graduated from the same schools and lived in the same areas. Instead of Lane as a last name, she was now Amanda Grant and her fake résumé said she'd worked as an executive assistant for the head of the New Jersey Port Authority, a subject with which she was familiar.

Hopefully no one would question her too closely. And when Hathaway's current assistant came down with a sore throat, the Shey Group had Amanda's name put on the top of the list at Hathaway's favorite temp agency. Bolstered by a designer suit Bolt had insisted she buy along with a new wardrobe for the job, she double-checked her jacket's lapel pin, with its microphone hidden inside so Bolt could hear every word.

This upcoming interview would be one of the riskier parts of the operation. Bolt couldn't be right there in the office with her until she'd first secured the job and saw to it that he was hired for security.

Palms damp, she pressed the elevator button to take her to Hathaway's suite. Bolt stood beside her as relaxed as if going for a stroll in Central Park. As agreed upon beforehand, they didn't speak. He would get off on the floor below and kill time, but would remain within panic-button distance. She fingered the electronic device in her pocket. She wasn't to press the button except for an emergency.

And he'd left the definition of what qualified as an emergency to her. If Hathaway came on to her, would she be able to keep the presence of mind necessary to fend him off? Of course she would. Now that she understood that Hathaway might employ the perfume bottle against her, she hoped to brace herself against the effects.

Besides, Hathaway couldn't come on to every woman in his employ or his empire would fall apart. Likely he wouldn't waste his power on her when he had all those supermodels to charm. So what if she'd caught his "look" at the party. Likely he hadn't meant to direct it at her and what had happened when she'd viewed the monitor could have been an unintentional side effect.

The elevator stopped and Bolt exited. Swallowing hard, Amanda watched him walk away. Not until she was alone did she realize how much she'd relied on his quiet strength to bolster her courage. She stroked her thigh, which held her holster and gun. Damn it, she was armed, ready, and she refused to think about failure. Or him. She couldn't afford distractions. She was here to do a job.

When the elevator rose to the next floor, she ignored the butterflies in her belly, ignored the perspiration beading between her breasts, ignored her watery knees.

Put yourself in the role. This is a job interview.

And Amanda had never applied for work without being hired. Still, she'd never requested work in such plush surroundings. Hathaway Balkmandy's Agency was a study in contrasts. Cold marble, high-tech desks, bright lighting and too many mirrors clashed with inviting apricot sofas and sunny-yellow pillows. The air was scented with aromatic cinnamon coffee and fresh pastries that added a sickening sweetness to her feelings of urgency.

Amanda gave her name to the receptionist and, with swift efficiency, the woman led her down a hallway with piped-in opera music to oversize stained-glass doors that allowed light in, while maintaining full privacy. Once she walked past those doors, she'd be on her own.

After declining coffee from the receptionist, Amanda squared her shoulders, raised her chin and hoped that with so many people around, Hathaway wouldn't try anything. With luck, he kept his carnal activities confined to his home.

At her entrance, Hathaway rose from behind a massive desk that was covered with files, a newspaper, computer, television and assorted pads of notes. He smiled warmly, his thinning hair revealing a shiny scalp.

"Please come in and have a seat, Ms. Grant. Can I get you coffee? Tea? A soda?"

"No, thank you. Please, call me Amanda."

She shook his hand, steeling herself against instant lust or at minimum an electric shock. But other than normal flesh, she noted nothing unusual. She waited to see if he'd mention her attending his party, but he didn't. Whether that meant he'd forgotten her or that he was an expert at hiding his thoughts, she couldn't be sure. She took a seat and pressed her knees together, then waited for him to speak.

She expected questions, but he pawed through the mess on his desk until he pulled out a file. "The temp agency said you could start immediately."

"That's correct."

"Good." He handed her a pad and a pen. "I need you to reschedule my luncheon appointment at the Russian Tea Room with Gerald Mino from today to Friday. Send flowers to…" He paused to peruse his desk again, and she wrote quickly, stunned that apparently the job was hers, and he expected her to start now. At least she didn't have to phone Bolt to let him know. He could hear everything from downstairs. "Flowers go to Lola Hegan at the Carlton Suites," Hathaway continued. "Phone agent Dennis Ringman and find out if he's booked the party planner for the spring show." She wrote and wrote, her hand steady as he gave her enough to do for a week. But she didn't ask questions. He had four secretaries that she could employ to mete out the assignments. Hopefully they recognized these people and could track down addresses and phone numbers.

When Hathaway stopped firing off orders, the office turned strangely quiet. She glanced up from her notes to find him frowning at her. "You were at my party the other night."

"Yes." Her heart skipped a beat but she kept a serene expression. "I was hoping to meet someone who could help me find work with your company."

"Why?"

"Because I need a job."

He shook his head, his eyes drilling her. "You misunderstood. Why did you pick *my* company?"

She hadn't prepared an answer for his question. But she'd always been able to think fast on her feet. "Actually yours isn't the only company on my list. When a friend hooked me up with the temp agency, I thought it would give me a chance to see where I best fit in. When you had an immediate opening, Hathaway Balkmandy's Agency went to the top of my list."

"Are you married?" He glanced at her ringless left hand.

She wanted the job, but she wouldn't let him walk all over her and his question was likely illegal. An employer wasn't entitled to ask such questions. "My personal business is my own."

"I may need you to work late nights and weekends."

She nodded, not trusting herself to speak. His tone was tough to read, but nothing weird seemed to be going on, except a boss testing his limits over a new employee.

"So if you have kids—"

"I don't."

"A boyfriend—"

"Not a problem."

He grinned with satisfaction. "That will be all for now, Amanda. I have a meeting here tonight at 10:00 p.m. I'll need you back here."

"At ten." She rose and exited his office before daring to take a breath, wondering what Bolt would think of the late-night meeting, but she remained so busy taking care of Hathaway's requests that she didn't have time for a coffee break, never mind dinner.

However, when she came out of the ladies' room at half past nine, she almost let out a yelp when a hand reached out of a nook and drew her behind potted plants. She had her gun drawn before she recognized Bolt's deep blue eyes. He wore a blond wig and mustache and had changed from a business suit into a casual shirt and jeans. A cap with the brim pulled low on his forehead completed the disguise.

"It's me," he whispered, his husky voice shooting a thread of longing into her gut. And this time, she fully believed the desire was all her own.

"Sheesh—" she reholstered her weapon and took care to straighten her full skirt "—you scared me."

"Sorry. I wanted to let you know that I've got a man replacing the night janitor. And I'll be downstairs so make sure you don't lose that pin."

"Thanks." She kept her tone low. "I've noticed nothing unusual, but I feel better knowing you are close by."

Bolt grinned. "Glad to know you have such confidence in me."

She patted her gun. "I should be able to take care of myself."

"No strange longings?"

She shook her head and his expression changed to disappointment. "I take it you were hoping that I might need your help?"

"Can you blame me?"

She stood on her tiptoes and kissed his cheek, taking advantage of the empty corridor. He smelled of mint and a citrus soap, a scent that reminded her of when she'd stood on the chair naked before him.

She almost hoped Hathaway used his strange power on her tonight so she'd have an excuse to do whatever she wanted with Bolt. She'd liked his kisses too much not to be tempted for more. She enjoyed his hands on her body too much to think they were done with one another. And she most definitely missed his arms wrapped around her too much not to appreciate them now.

She didn't want to ruin their plan by risking someone seeing them together and recognizing him later. So she told herself after her difficult afternoon and evening, she could satisfy herself with one long kiss and that would keep her going. Besides, most of the staff had left around seven o'clock.

Her lips shifted from his cheek to his mouth and he angled his head perfectly to capture her lips. My-oh-my the man could kiss. She closed her eyes and kissed him back, appreciating the way he revved her up faster than the caffeine kick from a triple espresso.

Seemingly of their own accord, her fingers followed

their own path over his shoulders and threaded into his hair. And she lost track of time as she focused on the rhythm of his tongue, the beat of his heart, the rush of excitement that elevated her pulse.

When he finally broke the kiss, she clung to him for another moment before forcing her hands to release him. As her good sense returned, she looked right, left, over her shoulder, but the corridor remained empty, allowing them a few more minutes of privacy.

"I don't like the sound of this late meeting." Bolt eyed her, his nostrils flaring from a mix of leftover heat from their kiss and suspicion of Hathaway.

"So far I haven't noted anything out of the ordinary," she admitted, expecting him to pounce on her admission.

And he did. "So our kiss was all your own idea?"

"You have a problem with that?" she countered, covering up her surprise that she had indeed initiated the kiss under her own volition. She wished she could wrangle another kiss but the elevator doors dinged.

People exited but walked the other way. Eyes warm and gentle, Bolt cupped her chin and ran his thumb over her bottom lip. "I'll never have a problem kissing you."

His words caused her muscles to go all warm and mushy. Pleased that he was as enthusiastic as she was, she nevertheless had to keep her mind on the fact they might only have these few minutes to converse. "You think Hathaway's going to try something tonight?"

"I'm not certain. His secretary's schedule says they are doing a photo shoot at 10:00 p.m."

"How did you—"

"I tapped into her computer when she left her desk."

Amanda frowned at him. The secretary's desk was in full sight of at least three others. "Someone could have seen you."

"I didn't tap in *from* her desk, but used a unit at another location."

"How do you know you didn't set off an internal alarm?"

"Because I'm good at what I do. I was taught by the best guy in the business." His lips tightened. "I'd wanted to wait until the day after tomorrow for Hathaway to find the bugs in his office during his normal security sweep, but I'm not leaving you alone with him that long. So the night janitor is going to knock over a chair and then you can find the bug and tell Hathaway he has a problem."

"Got it." She grinned at him. "Don't look so worried. I'll be fine."

"I don't like changing the plan. Hathaway's likely to be suspicious. The janitor will take off running, making him look guilty to take the heat off you. And a background check will lead back to Hathaway's usual security company so he won't want to use them to fix the problem."

"Understood."

"And if anything goes wrong—"

"I have my gun and the panic button."

People suddenly spilled into the corridor from two directions and she squeezed Bolt's hand then let go before taking the opportunity to walk away with a casual sway of her hips. But she couldn't help wondering if she'd told him the truth. Had that kiss been totally her own idea?

She believed so.

But could she be absolutely certain?

Exactly at 10:00 p.m. Amanda showed up at Hathaway's suite. With the double doors to his office propped open, she could see a beehive of activity inside and relief that she wouldn't be alone with him doused her with new confidence. A photographer had set up a backdrop, and lights with extension cords were taped to the floor. A makeup artist touched up one model's face while a hair stylist worked on a second model's locks. A third was busily peeling off a dress and no one seemed to notice her bare breasts as she changed into a bikini. Music blared from loudspeakers and two tall women wearing spiked heels and bikinis danced on Hathaway's desk which was now cleared of all paperwork.

Most agents didn't attend photo shoots but Hathaway kept close watch of his women. And apparently this was another shoot that included him with his models, but she had no idea why he wanted her there, too.

Behind the desk, Hathaway sat like a captain behind the wheel of his ship. A lit cigar smoked in his right hand, the other held what appeared to be scotch on the rocks. Another model stood behind him, one massaging his shoulders, while two others sat on the arms of his chair.

And despite all the noise and commotion, Hathaway's eyes fastened on her the moment she stepped through those doors. Again, she felt a powerful electric connection. Like a cobra awaiting prey, she was certain he was noting her expression and drawing his own conclusions regarding what she thought about his private party.

Oh, God. The same laser beam of desire that she'd felt at the party was back. Only this time it was five times stronger. Had he asked her here so she'd feel the pull of the perfume bottle? Was the ancient artifact close by? Her blood began to pound. Her breasts ached and it was all she could do not to tap her foot to the beat or sway her hips enticingly.

Think of ice.

Ice cubes.

Icicles.

Icebergs.

Damn. Thinking cold was doing nothing to relieve the increasing thrumming between her legs. Her breasts ached to be touched and her nipples hardened.

Pretending nothing was wrong and that she remained unaffected, careful to keep a smile pasted on her face and her eyes serene, she took a step in his direction. When he gestured for her to come closer, she edged toward his desk, careful not to step into the lights or block the photographer's lens. Hathaway patted his knee as if he expected her to take a seat on his lap.

No way. She didn't want to go closer for fear his power would increase. She gritted her teeth. *Look at his bald head. Look at his smarmy smile.*

She thought of Donna lying in the Dumpster but not even her grief could lessen the intensity of the lust coursing through her. Yet, the last thing she wanted to do was sit on Hathaway's lap.

Where the hell was the janitor?

She looked down at her attire as if to remind Hathaway she wasn't properly dressed in beachwear. A mistake. Hathaway snapped his fingers. Although the snap couldn't be heard above the techno music, one of the stylists responded and took her arm to draw her toward the rack of skimpy clothes.

"I'm not a model," she shouted.

"You are now. This cover is for *Fashion Deluxe* and it's featuring whatever Hathaway wants. Right now, he wants you, so let's get you dressed."

"No." She suspected this was Hathaway's move to get her closer to the bottle. From the almost irresistible pull of attraction, she wouldn't be surprised if he had it hidden right there in his desk. "I'm an executive assistant, not—"

"Hey." The photographer left his camera on the tripod and the lights ceased to flash. While the models took a short break, the photographer joined them, looking Amanda up and down as if she were a specimen on a lab table ready for vivisection. "I don't need another babe in a swimsuit. That skirt and blouse are perfect to counter all the bare skin." He instructed an assistant. "Put a steno pan and a pen in her hands and place her over there." Then he told Amanda, "And keep frowning at the rest of the group."

In moments she was standing under the hot lights in the designated spot with pad and pen. Holding still and fighting off Hathaway's magnetism caused perspiration to bead on her upper lip. One of the assistants dabbed at her with a napkin. Another sprayed something on her hair. A third fluffed out her skirt, and she barely turned in time to avoid the woman discovering her gun hidden in a thigh holster.

Any lingering questions she may have had about this whole crazy paranormal theory of Bolt's was put to rest when each rise and fall of her chest, each chafe of her lacy bra against her heated flesh, seemed to sensitize her breasts. Obviously she wasn't the only one feeling Hathaway's heat. The models were taking turns touching and stroking and kissing him. One of them had straddled his hips and gyrated her own, giving Hathaway a lap dance and an erection. Several models had lost their tops and the photographer was saying, "Go with it, ladies. Yes. Yes. Yes."

"You." He pointed at Amanda. "Get that dreamy look out of your eyes. Frown more. I want you to look upset. Angry. Disapproving."

Following his directions shouldn't have been so difficult. But she couldn't concentrate. The music seduced, swayed, serenaded. Her trembling knees fought to hold still. The fire in her loins simmered. Then, she noticed the janitor shuffle into the room and focused on him. He'd entered the room with a broom and a service cart and he went to empty the trash can.

Hold on. Just one more moment.

She'd never wanted to touch herself so badly.

She was moist, slick, aching.

But the janitor was about to make his move. Finally he stumbled, knocked over a chair and fell to his knees. And a piece of metal no bigger than a button zinged across the floor. Barely remembering her role, Amanda abandoned her position in the shoot and bent to pick up the tiny, round object. Then she motioned to a technician to cut the sound.

"Mr. Balkmandy?" Her voice shook.

"Call me Hathaway." His eyes bored into hers and she'd never wanted sex so badly in her life. It was as if every nerve ending was electrified. And even knowing that the rational part of her mind didn't like Hathaway wasn't enough to protect her. And the bastard knew it.

He was expecting her to say or do something to indicate how much she wanted him. His eyes glittered with triumph, and she shuddered, knowing how close she was to succumbing.

She held up the electronic bug. "That man—" she pointed to the janitor, who picked himself up and scooted toward the door "—tried to plant this under the chair."

The janitor fled, toppling his cart behind him to delay anyone from following.

"Stop him," Amanda shouted, pleased that the man had too much of a head start for anyone to catch him.

Then she turned to find Balkmandy was gripping her wrist, raising her hand that held the bug, eyeing her curiously. "You're just full of surprises."

Up close, his power seemed to wrap a haze of fire around her. She shook from need, longed to rip off her clothes and just barely controlled her trembling. Concentrating on the conversation was almost impossible. The fingers of her free hand caressed the panic button.

Hathaway had a pleased grin of satisfaction on his face as if knowing how badly she needed release.

No. She couldn't give in.

She depressed the panic button and gritted her teeth, praying Bolt would find a way to extract her. "Excuse me?"

The lines on his forehead creased with a frown. Hathaway pointed to her office. "We need to talk. Wait for me there."

It was all she could do to stagger down the hall and into the office he'd assigned her that morning. Bolt was already there, looking too good, too handsome, too male to resist, and she flung herself into his arms so hard she almost knocked him over.

His kiss was fierce, his hands insistent as he lifted her skirt and touched her right through her panties. Already swollen and sensitive, just one caress between her legs and she orgasmed. Gasping into his mouth, she would have fallen if he hadn't supported her with his free arm. And as the wave of pleasure crested and burst, she realized one orgasm wasn't going to be enough.

She hadn't released enough tension. Already she wanted more. That one release was like feeding a starving woman one bite of a meal. But there was no time for more.

She heard footsteps coming down the hall. "Hathaway's coming and I don't know if I can resist him."

"Don't worry. I'll take care of you," Bolt tried to re-assure her. Then in one smooth move, he shoved her into her chair and lunged under the desk. Then he rolled her forward until the chair arms hit the desk's top drawer and concealed him.

And not a moment too soon.

Hathaway eyed her with suspicion, but he still emit-ted that irresistible libido that was already sending her up in flames again. Eyes alert, mouth in a tight line, his voice was demanding. "How do you know what a bug is?"

Beneath her desk, Bolt ran his hands up her legs. Something cool pressed against her hip. And the band of her panty snapped free.

Oh, God. He must have cut the material with a pocket knife. And when he cut the other side and nudged her knees apart, she was totally bared to him. Open.

And if she revealed her shock to Hathaway, he'd be-come suspicious. Maybe find Bolt. She had to keep it together. Get a grip.

Hathaway couldn't see a thing below her waist, but he was frowning at her with such suspicion that she took a moment to recall he was waiting for an answer. "My former boss swept his office for bugs several times a week." Bolt's fingers had delved into her heat and she had no idea how she completed a sentence as delicious sensations coursed through her. "A few times we found devices like…"

She couldn't speak. Her fingers clenched and Hath-away's gaze dropped to her hands. She couldn't hold still. Not with Bolt's mouth plastered to her, his tongue flicking over her clit. She needed him so badly. And yet, this was insane. Hathaway was standing right there, watching her so closely, no way could she fool him. But she must or the mission would be a bust. She slapped one palm over her wrist to hold her hands still.

"What's wrong?" Hathaway demanded.

"I…feel…" *Oh. Oh. Oh.* Bolt's tongue expertly caressed her.

She was going to explode. Right in front of Hathaway.

But she couldn't or she might give away Bolt's presence. Her gut knotted. She tried to close her knees, but he had her pried wide open and his tongue never stopped.

Hathaway must have sensed that she was having trouble speaking. "You feel hot?"

"Yes."

"You're turned on?"

"Yes."

Oh my God. Bolt was driving her insane with his hands and lips and tongue. Her nipples were so hard, she ached. She was so tight, so ready to explode, that holding back was becoming less of an option by the moment. What was Bolt thinking? Did he plan for Hathaway to catch them?

No, he knew she was hot, and he was willing to risk the mission to prevent her from succumbing to Hathaway. But more was riding on her cover than recovering a precious antique. She wanted to clear Donna's name, and find her killer.

"So why haven't you approached me?" Hathaway demanded.

Even through her cloud of lust, Amanda knew he was suspicious as hell that she'd resisted and hadn't gone to him like all the other girls. "I don't…know you well enough…to…to…"

"You obviously want me." He glared at her and turned up the heat of his potent glance.

She broke into a sweat. No one could resist the pressure from both men. She was going to explode right in front of Hathaway. She knew it.

"I want you badly enough to come right now," she panted. She hoped he was egotistical enough to believe that he alone could send her over the edge without so much as a touch.

"Is that so?" Clearly pleased, he shot her a wolfish grin and his one hand clamped over both her wrists. "You don't even have to touch yourself?"

She gasped. Shook her head. With Hathaway gripping her hands and Bolt's face buried in her crotch, she was so trapped that she might as well have been bound hand and foot. And with the most delicious sensations arousing her, she couldn't hold back much longer.

"Please, let go of my hands. Leave."

"Not a chance." Hathaway leered at her. "I've never made a woman come like this. I want to see how much stronger I've become."

"Stronger?"

"Women have always been attracted to me."

Concentrating was almost impossible. But Bolt slowed the friction, just enough for her to maintain the conversation. "How do you do it?"

Hathaway laughed. "I don't give away my secrets. You want to learn them?"

"Yeah."

"Then you have to pay."

"How…much?"

"Let's just say, it's not money I want." His eyes glittered.

"What then?"

"When you come to me naked, on your knees, begging because only I can satisfy you, then—"

"It won't happen."

Apparently Bolt decided they weren't going to get any useful information out of Hathaway. Either that or he couldn't resist giving her what she so desperately needed. And within moments, the sensations heightened. The heat, the friction, all of Hathaway's mental pressure came to the boiling point and she exploded, her body jerking, her core pressing into Bolt's mouth, even as Hathaway held her hands still.

If she'd been free, she would have bolted out of the chair. The pleasure firing through her was that intense. But Bolt held her thighs down. She gasped and released a high-pitched scream.

She must have fainted because when she noticed her surroundings again, several people had run to her office in concern. Her scream must have drawn them there. Hathaway had released her hands and was eyeing her like a proud scientist over a successful experiment. The other women were already eager to draw him away.

The women and Hathaway had better things to do than stay with her, so they returned to the photo shoot. After they were gone, she sagged in her chair, too satiated to move, too stunned with what she'd done to even think clearly.

Gently Bolt rolled back her chair and climbed out from under the desk. One look at her and he knew she wasn't ready to speak. So he simply gathered her to him and rocked her gently against his chest, murmuring soothing words in her ear.

"You okay?" he asked.

"I may never be okay again. But you took a hell of a risk. Hathaway might have found you."

"He didn't." Bolt allowed the glow of approval in his expression to wash over her. He'd been certain she wouldn't blow the mission. If lives had been at stake, he might not have taken the chance he had—but no way in hell would he let Hathaway have her when his mission was simply to recover a priceless antique. He'd promised to keep her satisfied and he would be there for her—no matter the risk. Protective instincts he hadn't known he had were coming into play, making him determined to keep her out of Hathaway's unsavory hands. His explanation to Amanda was simple and true. "I trusted you to fool him and you did."

She tilted back her head and the dreamy satiation remained in her eyes. Satisfied that he'd pleased her, he planned to enjoy this mission more than any that had come before.

"But I'm not quitting," she said, her tone firm. "We're going to get that SOB."

"Yes. We are."

6

HATHAWAY BALKMANDY hadn't gotten to his position in life without taking risks. But he couldn't abide incompetence. After the photo shoot, he'd hired an investigator to do some fast detective work on the firm he currently used to sweep his agency for bugs, phone and computer taps. Only a few hours later he'd learned the agency had several questionable people on their payroll, one of them a dead ringer for the night janitor who'd disappeared right after he'd fled Hathaway's office. Hathaway regretted the man had gotten away before they could question him.

So his new executive assistant had been correct in her instant assessment that the janitor had been there for nefarious reasons. Hathaway liked her smarts. But most of all, the incident had left him curious about Amanda Grant.

Hathaway had always had a way with women, but he didn't understand them. He'd never understood how his mother forgave his father's drinking and cheating, or why she'd never reported him to the law whenever he'd beaten her and their only child. Hathaway remembered every bruise, every cut, every time he had to pretend he was like all the other kids in school. Concentrating on his studies had been almost impossible as he'd coped with the painful welts from a leather strap that had always found its mark no matter how much he'd tried to twist and turn out of the old man's grip. Hathaway hadn't been strong, but resentment and fury had fueled his cunning. At age sixteen when other kids were dreaming about fast cars and loose women, he'd arranged for his father to appear to have lifted a local drug dealer's stash.

Hathaway had never understood his mother's tears as she'd stood over his father's bloody body. She should have been glad her son had rid her of the man's mean fist, abusive cursing, sour breath. But was the bitch grateful? No.

When he'd confessed, telling her his clever plot, she'd turned *him* over to the cops. Hathaway had copped a plea and never looked back. He'd changed his name and become wealthy and famous. And when he'd heard that his mother had died, he'd felt nothing, no regret, no sadness, only satisfaction at knowing she'd gotten what she'd deserved for failing to protect him before he'd grown old enough to do it himself.

At least the bitch had been good for one thing. He'd learned that women were not to be trusted, but were simply to be used for his own purposes. The lesson had settled so deeply into his marrow that he had no fear that a woman could ever sink her hooks into him. And, oh, had they tried. Fame and wealth attracted the ladies like a magnet. Some women seemed sweet, others were obviously cunning, but they all wanted the same thing. Him.

But that wouldn't happen. He gave them sex, gifts and their fifteen minutes of fame, but he remained above all the petty emotions like love. Allowing the women to fawn over him, like the bitch never had, pleased him.

Hathaway's interest in the occult had led him to learn of the legends surrounding the perfume bottle. He'd spent a small fortune tracking the bottle to its former owner. And after he'd realized the perfume bottle would heighten his already considerable powers over women, he had to have it. When the owner wouldn't sell, he'd arranged for a thief to steal it. The price had been worth the risk. The perfume bottle had worked even better than expected.

Reverently Hathaway polished the old perfume bottle, taking care to buff the silver lace filigree along the top. Sometimes he wished the bottle could talk and tell him stories of its owners. What had they done with the bottle and how had they used its powers?

At first, Hathaway hadn't been able to control the strength over women the perfume bottle gave him. But slowly, he'd learned that using his power was like a sword, one that could cut both ways. It wouldn't do to have every woman in a room trying to screw him—that would cause suspicion. It would also disrupt his business. Women needed to keep their mind on their work, unless he required their services.

He also didn't want the world to suspect that his charms weren't inborn and natural. So he'd practiced until he could lower the intensity in public. Governing the heat factor was difficult and tricky and depended on his proximity to the bottle, which he took great care to keep safe and out of sight. So much seemed to be determined by factors outside his control, like the woman's nearness to him and the bottle, and how much of her attention was on him during those moments.

Recently he'd been practicing how to direct his powers and how to modulate the intensity without affecting the others in the room. So far, he'd only had partial success. But he would figure it out.

However, he wasn't certain he'd ever understand what had happened with Amanda Grant. If his power had been so strong to give her an orgasm without touching her except to hold down her hands, why hadn't she been begging for him to screw her like every other woman? Why had she been able to resist taking off her clothes and demanding that he service her?

The fact that she had orgasmed in front of him and yet resisted him was contradictory. Hathaway didn't like puzzles. If Amanda hadn't proven how useful she was, he might have simply fired her and replaced her with someone less complicated and problematical. But by pointing out the janitor's deceit, she'd helped Hathaway and he needed more of that fast-acting, clearheaded logic in his organization.

For now, he'd keep her around. Perhaps, Amanda was the perfect subject upon which to practice his control. The other women had ceased to be a challenge. Yes, one way or another, he would make good use of Amanda Grant.

IN EVERY OPERATION surprises arose. So far Amanda had handled this mission like a pro, but Bolt didn't like the worry he saw in her eyes now that they were back at the apartment. He admired Amanda's spunk and her courage. Since the moment she'd agreed to work with him she hadn't appeared to change her mind, even when things had gotten rough. He imagined what it must be like for her and squirmed a little.

Even if her file hadn't told him she liked to remain in charge, her personality would have revealed she wasn't the kind of person to yield to a paranormal power without seeing it as weakness. The tragedy of losing her parents and then having to raise her sister at a young age had made Amanda strong. And she'd coped by keeping her own emotions on the back burner, by keeping control and pursuing her goals.

So, he fully understood what inner strength it must take for her to make herself vulnerable to Hathaway and the bottle's powers. While she hadn't complained, he could see the constant tension in her eyes that wore a person down. She needed a break from Hathaway but with half the workweek still before her, she wouldn't get one. So he was very glad to settle her back in the luxury suite where he could soothe her.

From her file he knew her favorite wine was a Chardonnay and he'd already poured her a glass of one of the best years. Thanks to Kincaid's pull, he had a gourmet meal on the way from one of New York's best chefs.

He put on a Norah Jones CD, refilled Amanda's glass of wine and watched her sip appreciatively. "Good?"

"Yes, thanks."

She seemed formal, on edge, especially after that crazy scene under her desk. "If you want, you have time for a hot bath before the food arrives."

She tipped up her glass and downed a large gulp. "Sounds like a plan, but it would sound better if you'd join me."

His pulse accelerated at her words. "That's an invite I won't turn down. But you go on ahead and let me catch up. I need to call in and make a few arrangements."

"What kind of arrangements?"

"I want more people nearby, in case we run into a problem."

She kicked off her heels, padded over on bare feet and held out her empty glass. "I don't like the idea that other people will know what you and I are doing."

He poured her another drink. "They'll be close. But not that close."

"I suppose you know best." She eyed him above the brim of her glass. "I'd like to come out of this operation with a modicum of dignity. The fewer people who know what's going on, the better I'll feel."

Was she embarrassed that she couldn't control her lust? Even after two glasses of wine, he was having difficulty reading her. She didn't seem the slightest bit tipsy. In fact, she hadn't seemed to relax at all.

"Go on. Run the bath and I'll rub your shoulders."

Eyeing him with a weary, yet saucy heat, she nodded. "You're good at that."

"What?"

"Rubbing me." She grinned wider, saluted him with the glass and strolled toward the bathroom.

Apparently she wasn't annoyed at him for the stunt he'd pulled on her while under the desk. The entire situation had been risky and the operation would have been blown if they'd been caught. Yet, he'd rather have ruined the plan and found another way to recover the bottle than to have had Hathaway work his wiles on Amanda. Never before had Bolt's protective instincts for a partner been so strong. But going that far while he'd been under the desk had been necessary since she'd clearly been so needy. While he'd anticipated that she might chastise him afterward, if necessary he'd been prepared to accept her wrath.

Instead of anger, she'd given him attitude. He'd really lucked out when it came to Amanda for a partner. She might have been hesitant to accept this mission, but once she'd agreed, she was in all the way up to her perfectly arched eyebrows.

While Bolt could work with all different kinds of personalities, it was so much easier when everyone was on the same page. As he'd watched Amanda handle herself, his respect and admiration had increased until the lines between doing what was necessary for the mission and what he wanted personally had overlapped.

Bolt had no problem combining business and pleasure. As long as the pleasure didn't interfere with the mission, his boss wouldn't have any problems with the circumstances, either. But Bolt wasn't certain how Amanda felt. Was she separating the work sex from personal sex? Was he?

The mission goal and his own desires had merged until he was no longer certain of the reasons for his actions. Perhaps the nature of the mission had made his growing feelings for her inevitable. While he was no longer content for her to think of him as a means to an end and wanted her to desire him for himself, she remained all business.

However, he wasn't certain she knew her own mind. With Hathaway manipulating her, Bolt would be there for her when she needed him and not press her. He understood that giving up control was difficult for Amanda and while he suspected her feelings for Bolt might be deepening, she might not be ready to admit it—even to herself.

Amanda coped with life by keeping her emotions under a tight rein. When her parents had died, she hadn't had the luxury of falling apart. She'd had to raise a teenager, something many adults were unprepared to do. So she'd clamped down on her emotions and focused on her goals, her reaction determined and mature and brave. In many ways, Amanda reminded Bolt of so many of his Shey Group colleagues. She had the same stick-to-it drive and resolve to see the job through.

While it was his job to help Amanda, he wanted more. He wanted to take care of her. During a mission last year in Iraq, Bolt had to come to the aid of a British agent when they'd been trapped behind enemy lines while attempting to rescue a kidnapped Iraqi police chief. But his feelings for the British woman had never gone beyond friendship. With Amanda, he was downright possessive. After a trying day that had ended late, Bolt wanted to feed her and ensure she had a good night's rest. He was willing to do whatever Amanda wanted to help her through the mission. But he wouldn't be a red-blooded American male if he didn't think about her waiting for him in that tub. While he'd enjoyed every moment of satisfying her, his balls ached. He needed release, which if necessary, he could see to himself. But it would be so sweet to bury himself into her to the core.

However, that would be her call.

AMANDA RAN THE BATH and decadently poured a generous handful of hyacinth bath salts into the steamy water. After lighting several vanilla-scented candles, she turned off the light, shed her clothes and slid into the hot water with a sigh of satisfaction. She could get used to a tub like this, one with a heater that maintained the water temperature so the warmth wouldn't cool until she drained the tub.

Propping her head and neck on an air pillow, she closed her eyes and let the water cuddle her and coax away the tensions of her challenging day. Setting the jets to a soft, comfort spray, she leaned back and allowed the water pressure to massage muscles sore from tension. She supposed she should review what she'd learned, what she'd done and the shocking pleasure Bolt had given her. But she needed rest and her eyes closed as she drifted to a peaceful place.

She had no idea how long she napped, but when she

awakened, Bolt's hands were on her shoulders rubbing her neck. "Mmm. You feel great."

"I hated to wake you but the food will be here soon."

"If you keep working out all those knots, I may never get out of this tub."

He chuckled. "If you stay in there much longer, you'll turn into a prune."

She angled her head to watch him. "Do you like prunes?"

"Yeah." His eyes darkened with a sexual intensity that fully awakened her.

"So why haven't you joined me?" she complained.

"I was hoping you'd say that." He removed his shirt and his bronze muscles flexed, rippling in the candlelight.

Bolt had a great body, like an Olympic swimmer's, all lean, hard muscles that came from vigorous work-outs. She couldn't wait to slide her hands over his skin. She wanted to taste him, memorize him with her fingers and palms and lips and tongue. She wanted to breathe in his scent, run her fingers through his hair and over his jaw and neck and chest.

But as much as his masculine shape appealed to her, his words aroused her curiosity more. "You were wait-ing for my invitation?"

"Of course."

His easy admission had her almost sputtering in con-fusion. "But you didn't ask for permission when you... were under my desk."

"That was necessary. Tonight isn't." He slid next to

her in the tub until they touched at the shoulders, arm and hip.

"Hmm. You might be wrong." She didn't bother to disguise the teasing lilt to her tone.

Bolt stiffened. "You think Hathaway is still affecting you?"

"I haven't had sex in a long time, and perhaps that makes me more sensitive to his power of suggestion or the bottle or whatever the hell he uses."

"I hadn't considered that angle."

"Well…then it's a good thing I did." She slid her hand along his thigh. "Because I want to make love tonight and maybe if we do it right, I'll be immune to Hathaway tomorrow."

"There's a wrong way to make love?" Bolt joked casually. But even if the huskiness of his tone hadn't revealed his interest in her, she couldn't miss his very prominent erection.

"I like to have the choice. When Hathaway creates such strong unnatural needs, I don't feel like myself."

"When you're with Hathaway, I can't give you that control. But I can do so now."

"What do you mean?"

"That we can do nothing…or whatever you like. I'm at your complete command—after all, it's only fair for you to take charge for a change."

His magnanimous offer took her breath away and her enthusiasm escalated. She tested him. "Right now, I don't want you to move one muscle." Her hand cupped him where he was soft, and she trailed her fingers upward to where he was hard. "Nix that. You can move one muscle, but only one muscle."

"Are you certain?" he asked.

"Certain that I want you? Yes. Certain making love will protect me from Hathaway? No. But I can't think of a better way to learn how to counter him, can you?" She trailed her fingers over the ridge of his sex and watched a corded muscle in his neck throb.

"I can't think at all. All the blood seems to have left my brain."

She laughed. "For what I have in mind, thinking isn't necessary."

Sitting up, she changed position until she kneeled between his thighs. Picking up several handfuls of bubbles and water, she poured it over his chest, enjoying the sight of the trickles running down the hard ridges and defined muscles, the water droplets clinging to his tight nipples. Leaning forward, she nuzzled his neck, breathed in his scent and marveled at the wonderful texture of his flesh. The man had great skin, tanned and toned and firm and slick.

She finally had the opportunity to touch him the way she wanted and, true to his word, he held perfectly still. She liked having him at her mercy for once. And she planned to make the most of the opportunity, especially when she noted the tension in his mouth, the narrowed eyes that told her that remaining still was oh-so difficult for a take-charge man like him.

But the fire in his eyes encouraged her to give him a taste of what it felt like to burn until every thought was devoted to attaining only one thing—release. She'd known that feeling all too well recently. And now he would know it, too.

Leaning forward, she brushed her lips over his, purposely skimming her nipples across his chest, and ignoring his jutting sex. She wanted him to guess where and how and when she would touch him next. She wanted him straining. She wanted him on edge. She wanted to see how far she could push him for a change, and her curiosity had nothing to do with the mission. Her interest was all her own.

What she hadn't counted on was that touching him would cause her pulse to elevate, her breath to hitch and her breasts to ache. Touching him had become intimate and personal because only her own wishes motivated her—not some damn bottle. A pleasant tingle between her thighs intensified as she stroked his shoulders, skimmed a path down over his hard belly and then dipped to his sex.

"Tell me you want me to touch you there," she demanded and pulled her hands upward.

"Touch me," he rasped.

She turned a bottle of lotion upside down and then dunked her hands under the water. Grasping him with both hands, she watched his eyes as she moved her fingers up and down ever so slowly. His hands clenched the side of the tub. A groan of pleasure guided her to a sensitive spot directly under his swollen head.

"I can't take…much more." His words were half warning, half promise.

"You'll take whatever I decide to give," she whispered, feeling strong and feminine.

She liked that he wanted her this much. She liked that he didn't think he could maintain control. She liked driving him right to the brink.

And it was good to know that sex with this man didn't always have to be burning-up desperation, that she could build the fire slowly, enjoy each flicker, each catching ember. She had no doubts that soon she would finally have him inside her. But she would control the moment, the tempo and rhythm. And she appreciated that he wanted to please her—to the point of holding back his own pleasure.

Oh, yeah. Her hands continued to tease him, but she didn't apply enough pressure for him to explode. She wanted to save that moment for when he was inside her.

"Kiss me," she commanded. She leaned forward and slanted her mouth over his, giving him no choice but to accept her tongue, to yield to her fingers playing with his sex, to submit to her nipples taunting his chest as their mouths fused.

Lifting her hips, she meant to straddle him and finally have him inside her. But he tore his mouth from hers. "Condom. By the faucet."

That he'd remembered, and she hadn't, startled her, although it shouldn't have. She hadn't been herself since she'd met this man, but now she couldn't blame the bottle. Her wants and lust were all her own. Fumbling for the packet, her fingers shook. The slippery soap made ripping the foil impossible and she grunted in aggravation.

BOLT TOOK IN her expression, the way her nose squinched up, the way her lips pouted and it took every brain cell he had to remain still. "Want some help?"

"I can do it."

"My hands are dry."

"Fine." She held the condom out to him by the edges to keep it dry, but the moment he took it, her hands delved back under the water and locked on to their target.

While he damned sure wasn't going to complain, her seeking fingers made the immediate opening of the packet even more of an urgent matter. After a few days of Amanda's company, he felt ready to burst, but he refused to climax until he was certain she would be right there with him. So he remained on that painful edge, appreciating her every sensual stroke. When he couldn't take another moment, he ripped the foil.

But she tugged on his sex, her tone ardent and hoarse. "Kneel."

He did as she asked and when he finally projected out of the water, she splashed away the suds. He expected her to take the condom and sheathe him or allow him to do so, but instead, she took him into her mouth. Instant pleasure rammed home. The exquisite pull of her lips combined with her busy tongue and fierce heat caused every cell in his torso to fire and demand that he pump his hips. But with her hands tugging on his balls, she held him captive.

And when he gently tried to withdraw in order to increase the friction, she nipped him and squeezed where he was most sensitive, warning him not to move.

Yet the pressure from her tongue and lips was driving him wild.

Building tension had him strung so tight that he had to brace his hands against the side of the tub. His breath came in hungry, hot gasps. Surges of electric bliss centered in one area.

He was losing control, yielding in splendid wonder to her expertise. His muscles clenched, ready to explode. "I'm going to—"

"Not yet." She clamped down at the base of his sex, stopping his ejaculation.

His heart pounded and he broke into a melting sweat. He'd never been so hard, so engorged, so needy, so close. His ears rang. Amanda's sheer enthusiasm had him excited to the max. Just one flicker of her tongue, one caress from her palm would shoot him into ecstasy.

He had no idea when he'd closed his eyes but when he opened them, she had a satisfied glow on her face, a wicked gleam in her eyes and a knowing twist to her lips. "Was that the doorbell I just heard?"

"Doorbell?" He was having trouble concentrating.

She laughed. "Didn't you say something about food being delivered?"

He said the first thing that popped into his head. "I can't answer the door in this condition."

The bell rang. This time he heard it clearly. And he didn't give a damn about food right now. The only hunger he wanted to fulfill was his hunger for her.

She stood, the bubbles and bath water gleaming off

her skin in the candlelight. "I'll answer the door and be right back. But you have to promise me something."

He could barely think and she wanted promises. Hell, he'd promise her anything if she'd return and keep doing what she'd been doing.

"What?" he growled, starting to sit back into the water.

"Wait for me."

"Okay."

"Stay exactly like that." She challenged him with a look, running one finger down his chin. Then she stepped from the tub and slipped into the bathrobe that was hanging on the back of the door, slowly covering her gorgeous body.

"You want me to wait for you in this position?" He was on his knees, his hands braced on the rim, his sex aching, his blood simmering. But he knew she was getting off on taking back a measure of control. He wanted to give what Hathaway had taken away. Even if he'd never gone so far before, he was willing to do so for her.

"I like the idea of you waiting for me." She knotted the belt at her waist.

"And you're worth waiting for," he admitted, already counting the seconds until her return.

"There's one more thing."

"Yes?"

She bent to kiss him, and the V at the neck of the robe parted, showing him once again exactly what he'd be waiting for.

Her scent caressed him and then he realized she wasn't going to kiss his mouth but the tip of his sex. That one final lick he'd needed to shoot him over the edge was no longer enough. She'd given his ardor a well-timed moment to cool. So now the sweet lick was just enough to tease and taunt and torment.

"When I return, I'm going to touch you someplace I haven't already explored," she promised with a silky huskiness that left him intrigued. The sensual promise of her words, combined with a final stroke of her hand, had him rock-hard and right back on the edge. "Think about how much fun we're going to have when I return."

Fun? He was so wound up, he wanted to roar with frustration. It would be so easy to snap. To rise to his feet, take her up against the counter, or the door, or tug her back into the tub and give them what they both wanted. But even through his pounding desire, he understood that's not what she needed. She couldn't succumb to the effects of the perfume bottle repeatedly without it beating down her spirit. She didn't want to always be the recipient, always be the one whose need was so strong that she'd do anything for release. So she wasn't simply giving him a taste of what it felt like to be so needy, she was trying to find a balance.

And he would give that to her. Because he could. Because he wanted to. Because she was worth waiting for. If she was strong enough to put up with Hathaway, then he'd be strong enough to wait for…whatever she wanted.

And even as he wondered where she intended to explore next, he already suspected. And the woman was playing with fire.

She returned in less than a minute but his imagination was raging like a class-five, whitewater river, frothing and twisting and turning. After she slipped from the robe, his gaze roved over her in appreciation. He liked her lean belly and tight butt and he also liked that she wasn't skin and bones. When he held her she felt like a woman, not a girl. And he wasn't afraid she'd break.

"Miss me?" Her eyes sparkled and she clearly held something in her closed fist, yet he couldn't determine what, either from her secretive grin or from a hard look at her hand. But she was obviously pleased with herself.

"Of course I missed you," he ground out.

"Good. Don't move."

"Okay." He hoped his voice sounded as if he wasn't in danger of grabbing her.

She trailed her fingers in the water, creating waves that lapped at him hungrily, and she grinned when his sex leaped, telling her he was more interested than ever. But how could he not react that way at the sight of her lovely breasts, slender waist, curvy hips and plump thighs? Yum. He recalled her taste, her own special flavor as she'd come into his mouth.

Now, she was in control, and this was a different kind of excitement. She stepped to the side and he turned his head to follow her.

"Eyes forward," she commanded and then walked behind him. The little minx. What was she up to? He could no longer see her, but her shadow on the wall and the splash of water on his thigh told him she'd stepped into the tub.

She nipped his neck, wound her hands around his

waist and played with his nipples. The bites on his neck combined with her twisting pressure on his nipples followed by soothing licks was a new form of torture. He wanted her to touch his sex, but she ignored that part of him. Instead she nibbled his earlobe and her fingers traced a simmering slide to his buttocks.

"Spread your knees wide."

When he complied, she drizzled bath oil over his chest, his stomach and pelvis. The oil slithered and clung to his flesh. Her touch was so light, so airy. He needed heat and pressure and she was driving him insane with need.

He braced his arms on the rim, determined not to move. When she let more oil spill onto his back and buttocks, he noted she took special care to make sure she didn't miss a spot. And then her fingertips began to massage the oil into his body. She started with his chest and he'd never known his nipples could be so sensitive. Ever so slowly, she dipped lower and his breath seemed to halt in his lungs.

And when her fingers finally closed over him and she pumped her hand up and down, slowly, with too little pressure for him to find relief, he knew both unimaginable pleasure and ultimate frustration. He was burning for release and determined not to reveal how close he was.

Consumed by the raging, all-out need to finish, he craved more. He was so close. Aching. Ready. But she must have sensed his urgency because she released her hold of him and began to caress his back and shoulders.

He groaned in sheer exasperation.

"Hold on a bit longer," she encouraged. "I'm not done with you yet."

She explored his shoulders and back and then the insides of his thighs. And finally, she caressed his buttocks, moving closer and closer to the sensitive area between his cheeks. The suspense of what she would do, the anticipation, had him agitated and excited and intrigued.

"Brace yourself," she warned. And then she reached around to pump his sex, but at the same time, she placed something icy cold into him. And he went off in an explosion, so fast, so hard, that he saw stars. He shouted with the joy and beauty of fire and ice. She didn't let go, kept up the heat in front, the ice in back, prolonging the pleasure until, totally spent and satiated, he sat back on his heels.

She cradled him with her body and he tilted his head back against her shoulder. She held him for a long time, and when he finally returned to his full senses and recovered an awareness of his surroundings, he couldn't believe that she'd given him so much and taken nothing for herself.

Give him a hot meal and a bit of sleep and he'd be ready to show her exactly how much she was beginning to mean to him. Being with her had become more to him than simply a pleasurable mission. His feelings had gone from waiting to have a good time to truly caring for her. He was starting to think he wanted a relationship with Amanda Grant beyond being partners.

However, he had his work cut out for him. How did he get her to notice him beyond the confines of the mission? She was so focused on her goal that making her see him as a man in her life would not be an easy task.

However, Bolt was certain he could rise to the challenge.

7

AMANDA HAD JUST EATEN the last bite of the leftover chocolate mousse when her cell phone rang. Odd. Who would be calling at this early hour of the morning. When she checked the caller ID, she almost hung up thinking it was a wrong number. Yet, something about the name, Melanie Carter, sounded familiar.

So Amanda flicked open her cell phone. "Hello."

"Amanda Lane?"

A shiver raced down Amanda's spine. No one was supposed to know her real last name. "This is Amanda Grant."

"I'm Melanie Carter, a friend of Donna's. I used to be a model."

Melanie? The name sounded familiar. Amanda recalled her sister mentioning a friend whom she met for lunch. However much she might want to talk to Melanie about Donna, Amanda had to remember her cover.

"I'm sorry. You must have the wrong number."

"You're Donna's sister. I recognized you from the picture she always carried in her wallet."

Amanda was so busted. Her expression must have

shown that the entire mission was at risk because Bolt lost his sleepy-eyed look and the charming grin. His eyes narrowed and he moved to her side of the table.

Amanda saw no point in denying the truth of her identity when the woman had seen proof that she was Donna's sister. "Why are you calling me?"

"This is probably a really bad idea...I'm so scared." She stopped and took a shaky breath. "But I owe it to Donna to meet you. Be at the corner of 5th Ave and 42nd Street in an hour."

The phone clicked in Amanda's ear. Stunned, she repeated Melanie's words to Bolt. "Was I wrong to admit I'm Donna's sister? She could blow my cover to Hathaway."

He shook his head. "This woman obviously knew who you were. Lying would have done no good. And if she'd wanted to report you to Hathaway, she'd already have done so. Besides, if she thinks she owes Donna, maybe she's on our side."

"Maybe," Amanda whispered, knowing that despite her escalating heartbeat, no way was she going to miss this opportunity. If Melanie had been telling the truth, she might give Amanda some clues to what had happened to her sister. "We have to meet her."

"Yes, but we'll take precautions."

She could have kissed Bolt again for agreeing. Most men wouldn't want to take the risk. But Bolt was willing to risk his mission of finding the perfume bottle for her own goal of finding her sister's killer. His only stipulation was that they be careful and she agreed wholeheartedly. "If my sister knew this Melanie well enough to show her my picture, she might have information about Hathaway that we can use."

"How did Melanie sound on the phone?" Bolt asked, heading for the surveillance room with the security monitors. Once there, he booted his computer.

"Scared." She trailed behind Bolt and wasn't the least bit surprised when he took her phone and typed the caller's number into his computer, which revealed a downtown pay phone located in a subway station.

With surprising ease, Bolt found data on her caller. "Melanie Carter was a professional model, until a car accident ruined her career."

"Was she scarred?" Amanda guessed.

Bolt's fingers sprinted across the keyboard and he pulled up medical records in an astonishingly short period of time, revealing how accomplished he was at Internet searches. "Whiplash caused a neck injury and she now suffers from vertigo."

"So how did she and my sister meet?" Amanda wondered out loud.

"One of the Shey Group people has a fantastic program that might help. I already have it running for matches between Melanie, Hathaway and your sister. The system tracks their birth place, grade school and medical records, health clubs, etc. for any common places they might have met. However, we probably won't have an answer until tomorrow."

"That's amazing."

He shut down the computer and stood. "We need to

have the street corner scoped out." He flicked open a phone. "I'm calling in help. Why don't you dress?"

She nodded, uncertain if he wanted to hurry her along or if he didn't want her listening to his conversation. But her focus was on Melanie's information. Amanda couldn't recall her sister saying much about Melanie. Amanda and Donna had chatted more about her career change and Hathaway than her friends. But, Donna always had a group of acquaintances around her, women who admired her looks and brains.

As Amanda dressed, she tried to think about finding out what had happened to her sister rather than what she and Bolt had shared earlier. She wasn't certain what had come over her. She wasn't usually so free, so uninhibited and creative. Either Bolt brought out the vamp in her, or she was suffering the aftereffects of exposure to Hathaway's unusual powers. As she slipped on a silk blouse, she put those thoughts out of her mind. She refused to let what had happened between them distract her from her mission.

Amanda quickly changed into the business clothes she'd chosen. Wearing a skirt, her gun in easy reach in her thigh holster, she ran a brush through her hair and applied lip gloss before Bolt returned to his room.

Within moments, he dressed in navy slacks, a dark shirt and jacket. But arming himself took longer. He wore a gun at the small of his back, another at the ankle. He placed a switchblade in his pocket and clipped several throwing stars to the inside leather of his belt. The casual manner in which he armed himself was efficient, automatic, yet careful.

"You think we're walking into danger?" she asked, hoping her curiosity wouldn't hurt his chances of retrieving the bottle. And yet, finding her sister's killer had to take priority.

"We're walking into the unknown. I assume you're armed?" His eyes locked with hers and she read his concern.

She nodded. Knowing he would protect her made her feel safer. Bolt might be willing to risk danger but he wasn't foolish enough to go in without preparation. "You think Melanie had something to do with my sister's death?"

"Unlikely, but possible. Frankly I'm more concerned that Hathaway might be following Melanie than I am that Melanie's in collusion with him."

"I hadn't thought of that." She fired an admiring glance in Bolt's direction. "So what do you want me to do?"

"Just be yourself. Ask lots of questions." He frowned and she knew something was bothering him.

"What?"

"The less Melanie knows about us and our mission, the less she can give away."

"And?"

"It's not wise for Melanie to meet me. She may back off if you don't come alone. So I'll stay in the shadows and cover you."

"Fine." She couldn't think of a better man to cover her back, or her front, or her... Sheesh! Was it the effect of the bottle or the man himself that had her thinking about sex at a time like this?

Bolt was definitely special. She'd never forget his determination to let her have her way. The powerful impression he'd left was permanently branded into her brain, his taste and scent distinctive and wondrous. Yet, his attitude now meant as much.

Amanda wasn't accustomed to fieldwork, and yet, he wasn't lecturing her or automatically taking the lead. Bolt respected her enough to let her conduct the interview as she saw fit, and his confidence that she could handle herself made her feel not merely good, but great.

But he hadn't lost any of his protective instincts. His reminder was gentle. "You still have the lapel pin?"

"Yeah." She went to the drawer and pinned it on her blouse so Bolt could listen to her conversation with Melanie. Although he hadn't given her instructions, he knew more about this kind of operation than she did and it would be foolish to pretend otherwise. "Any tips?"

"Don't agree to go anywhere with her. Don't take any chances. Trust your gut."

His serious demeanor coupled with his faith in her caused her throat to tighten and her hands to tremble. To hide her reaction, she shoved them deep into her jacket pockets. But then she glanced over to Bolt. He wore a cocky grin and she immediately felt silly for worrying. He was big, strong and armed to the teeth.

What could go wrong?

BOLT MERGED INTO the shadows, hating that Amanda stood so exposed on the corner under a street lamp. New York City never shut down, even late at night. But the traffic was light with few pedestrians passing by, making her an easy target. Although the Shey Group had sent a team ahead to scout out the location and they'd found nothing suspicious, there was no way he could protect her completely. A drive-by shooter, a sniper in any of the myriad of buildings could have her in his sights and pull the trigger before Bolt's team spotted a problem.

Yet, Bolt had known from the expression in her eyes that he wouldn't have been able to talk her out of coming. She was too determined. And Amanda wasn't a woman to refuse to follow a lead out of fear for her safety. She would have gone with or without him. And while he admired her courage and understood her reasoning, he would have much preferred if she'd chosen to remain with him at the apartment. Not just because their evening had been interrupted, but because she would have been safe.

He glanced at his watch. Melanie was late. Amanda waited on the corner, still and steady, not even glancing his way. When a woman came rushing down the block, Bolt used his miniature binoculars. Even in the darkness, he recognized Melanie from his computer search. Tall and willowy, she no longer moved like a model. She limped and held her head at an odd angle as if every step caused pain. Bolt recalled the car accident that had ended her career and wondered how she supported herself now. He'd found no other data on her, no investments, no property owned, not even a driver's license. But she was also clean, with no criminal record.

Bolt watched the woman who didn't hesitate, walking directly to Amanda. Their conversation carried clearly to Bolt through his receiver.

"You look just like your picture," Melanie said.

"I was Donna's only family," Amanda admitted, her voice had the right touch of friendliness to encourage the other woman to talk. "I raised my sister after our parents died and I miss her so much. How did you meet?"

"At a fund-raiser. Since my accident most of the other models have avoided me, as if car accidents are contagious, or perhaps they just don't want to think about how even a short career can end so fast. But your sister was always kind. We met for lunch once a week, whenever her schedule permitted, and I always enjoyed her conversations about the business. I'd become jaded. She was still fresh and enthusiastic and reminded me of another time."

"You must have meant a lot to Donna if she confided in you."

"She didn't. Not exactly. But I thought you'd want to know that before her death, she was scared."

"Of what?"

"She didn't specify. In her own way, she was private. But she once mentioned that someone might be following her."

"A stalker?"

Amanda really had an instinct for this kind of work, Bolt noted. She obtained answers by invoking Melanie's sympathy and trust—not an easy goal to accomplish considering the circumstances. Melanie was clearly antsy, shifting from foot to foot, awkwardly looking over her shoulder as if she expected an attack at any moment.

Although Bolt listened carefully to the conversation, he automatically swept the street in both directions. A homeless man pushed a shopping cart into an alley. Several early risers—businessmen wearing suits and juggling briefcases, coffee and cell phones—walked briskly by, ignoring the two women.

When Bolt realized he'd tensed every muscle, he had to force himself to relax. If trouble arose, he would do Amanda no good if he was so tight he couldn't move. And even as he assessed the vicinity, he recognized that his feelings for Amanda were as broad as the sidewalk. It was normal to worry over the safety of his partner, but his concern for Amanda went beyond normal bounds. He was very aware of her every expression and mood, and wondered why he cared so much.

The women's discussion jerked him back to the moment. Melanie's tone was hurried and hushed. "Donna didn't say who was following her."

"But you think she knew him?"

"Maybe. She didn't even say if the person was male or female, but she wouldn't have been frightened by a woman. When I suggested she call the police, she refused and mentioned a problem at work. At the time, I thought she was changing the subject, but now I'm not so certain that work and whoever was following her weren't connected."

"What kind of problem did she have at work?"

Amanda sounded both patient and curious, but Bolt's impatience was escalating. Melanie seemed to be stalling. Either that or she was a very poor storyteller, and he wished she'd get to the point.

Melanie took a moment to remove a hanky from her pocket and blow her nose. "Donna wanted to model full-time, but Hathaway wasn't giving her enough look-sees—going out to visit photographers and clients with the hopes of impressing them to gain a job. She thought Hathaway might be holding her back."

Bolt hoped the handkerchief wasn't a signal to someone else and kept careful watch. A bus rolled by. Taxis seemed to be switching shifts and the blackness of night started to ebb into a dirty gray dawn.

"I don't understand." Amanda remained calm. "Hathaway's agency earned a commission every time Donna modeled. Wouldn't he want to find her all the work she could handle?"

"Apparently Donna had overheard a conversation where a client specifically asked for her. Hathaway told them Donna was busy that day—but she wasn't."

"So you have no proof that the person following her was connected to work, only your suspicions?" Amanda asked.

Melanie shrugged. "I'm just guessing. I could be wrong, but I'd thought you'd want to know, especially about Hathaway's diary. Donna told me he wrote everything in it. Perhaps there's incriminating evidence."

"Did Donna say where he kept this diary?"

Melanie shook her head.

"Why couldn't you tell me about my sister on the phone?"

"Donna made me promise to be careful. She'd heard odd clicks on her phone, believed someone might be opening her mail, and then she was dead. I spoke to a lawyer and he said not to bother the police. I didn't have any real evidence to help them solve Donna's murder. And—"

"And?"

"I didn't want to get involved," Melanie sounded torn, guilty but frightened. "If someone believes that I know more than I do, they might decide to kill me, too."

Amanda hugged the other woman. "I understand. Thank you for meeting me. Could you tell me one other thing?"

"If I can."

"Do you know if my sister showed my picture around Hathaway's office to anyone else?"

Good question. Clearly Hathaway was in the dark about Amanda's identity, otherwise he probably would have confronted or simply refused to hire her. But someone else at the company might recognize her as Donna's sister and tell Hathaway. Knowing how easily her cover could be blown made Bolt uneasy. He didn't like depending on Melanie's silence to keep Amanda safe—but what choice did he have? Vowing to redouble his vigilance, he perused the street but saw nothing of concern.

"I don't know if she showed around the picture or not. But I haven't said a word to anyone."

Melanie's statement only partially reassured him.

She could easily be lying, setting a trap. Trusting Amanda's safety to a stranger rubbed him wrong. And yet, Bolt had been in this business long enough to know that help could come from unusual sources.

"Thanks. Is there some way to get in touch with you if I have more questions?"

Melanie shook her head again. "It's too dangerous. I'll contact you. And if you find the diary, I'd like to know if it helps you." Melanie briskly turned and limped away.

Bolt didn't totally relax until he and Amanda were digging into breakfast at the corner diner. Something was niggling at the back of his mind. His gut told him the meeting was a setup, but he had yet to discern what had his hackles up. He hoped the tail he now had on the mysterious Melanie would unearth something.

Perhaps his growing protectiveness toward Amanda was to blame. She'd lost her parents and now her sister. He would make damn sure she didn't suffer another blow.

He ordered coffee, a toasted bagel with cream cheese, lox, capers and onions. Amanda preferred a Western omelet with orange juice and coffee. He appreciated that she didn't chatter, giving him time to contemplate her conversation with Melanie, but by the time the food arrived, he had yet to figure out what was wrong.

Amanda dug into her food with enthusiasm and he enjoyed watching her eat. Too often women picked at their food and pushed it around their plate but never seemed to put any in their mouths. Amanda, however, ate with a delicate and enthusiastic sensuality. He liked watching her lift a bite to her lush lips. He enjoyed her satisfaction as she tasted her food and swallowed.

"The coffee's heaven." She eyed him over the brim of her cup.

"Breakfast is my favorite meal of the day."

She raised a speculative eyebrow at his partially eaten food. "The bagel's not to your liking?"

"The food's fine, but something about Melanie's bothering me." He lifted the bagel, bit and chewed, the odd combination of flavors one that he hadn't tried until another Shey Group operative who'd grown up in New York turned him on to it. He loved the food in New York and the city's vibrancy, so different from the slower pace of home.

"Melanie didn't grovel over Hathaway as every other model does."

"That's it!" Bolt swallowed the last bite of his bagel. "You're brilliant."

"I am?" She grinned and then rubbed her brow as if she had no idea what he was talking about. "I didn't want to push it by asking Melanie about Hathaway. She was spooked enough as it was."

"Well, at least it seemed as though she isn't in collusion with Hathaway. Otherwise he would know your identity."

"Maybe he does know." She shivered. "Maybe he's waiting to kill me as he did Donna."

"If he knows your identity, he will never hire me. But if he offers me the job, we'll know your cover is still good." Bolt was certain of that much. "I think your cover is safe for now. But I get the feeling Melanie's hiding something and using us for her own purposes. She sure wants us to find his diary."

"Maybe he wrote about Melanie in it."

"That makes sense. I'd be willing to bet my next paycheck that Melanie was just as affected by Hathaway as every other woman, but after her accident she couldn't get near him. A man like Hathaway surrounds himself with beautiful, successful people. Hathaway wouldn't want to be seen or photographed with Melanie. The man's all about his image."

She ignored the cup of coffee in her hand. "So you think Melanie was living vicariously through my sister? That she pretended to listen to Donna's modeling stories when in reality she wanted to hear about Hathaway?"

"Maybe." Bolt frowned. "We need to go deeper into Melanie's background. She seemed way too eager for us to find that diary, as if she has reasons of her own to hate Hathaway and wants us to do the dirty work. But we need to be careful. I don't trust Melanie or her information."

"Okay." Amanda checked her watch. "But if I don't want to be late, I need to leave for work."

BOLT DIDN'T HAVE an opportunity to talk to Amanda in private until they met on the roof for lunch. He handed her a corned beef sandwich with sauerkraut on rye bread and a dill pickle. "Hope you have a breath mint."

"Who cares?" She bit into the sandwich. "Delicious."

Since she hadn't pressed the panic button, Bolt assumed she hadn't been around Hathaway this morning.

And he was still waiting for the phone call to summon him to check Hathaway's security.

Amanda sipped from a diet soda. "You look happy with yourself."

"I did more research on Melanie Carter. She and Hathaway were once an item."

"Now that's interesting." Amanda cocked her head to the side. "That might help confirm your theory that Melanie was more interested in Hathaway than my sister's modeling career."

"I haven't told you the best part."

"What?" Her eyes brightened in anticipation.

"Hathaway supports Melanie. After deep digging we found a connection between one of his subsidiaries and checks to Melanie."

"Was he involved in the car accident?"

"No. He was in Milan at the time."

"And they never married or had a child?"

"No."

"Maybe they're friends."

"I don't think so. Here's the strange part. There are no records of any phone calls between them. If they were friends, or if he was paying her out of kindness, we should have found something."

"Hathaway doesn't seem the type to be quietly charitable. If he was giving her money on the up and up, he'd want publicity for helping an injured ex-model."

"True," Bolt agreed.

"I don't understand why Melanie mentioned the diary. It's almost as if she wants us to search Hathaway's private quarters. But what could be in a diary that's so important to her?"

He shrugged. "Since we're searching for the bottle, it won't hurt to look for the diary as well. If he has a bedroom safe, he might keep the diary and the perfume bottle there together. If we get in, maybe we'll both find what we're after."

Bolt finished his sandwich. Food tasted better around Amanda. The sky seemed bluer, even on an overcast day. And out here on the roof, she looked wonderful.

Bolt wasn't eager to find the perfume bottle. That would mean their working together would come to an end. As much as he worried about her being alone with Hathaway, he needed more time with Amanda. Time to figure out what he wanted from her.

But how?

While the mission had to come first, Bolt was determined to make the most of their time together. And later, he'd simply have to use his ingenuity to ensure they had a chance to work out what they wanted from each other.

Her cell phone rang. "Hello?" She signaled Bolt with a thumbs-up and a wide smile. "Yes, sir. I know a security expert. He used to work for my former boss. I'll give him a call and see if he's available."

Bolt loved a good plan. And Hathaway had just bitten into the bait. Now all he had to do was hook him and reel him in.

8

AMANDA RETURNED to Hathaway's office with a plan to try to befriend a few of Hathaway's models in the hope of finding out gossip about the agent and Melanie. But the newer models were too busy to chat and the more experienced ones didn't deign to speak with Hathaway's executive assistant unless they wanted something.

So Amanda bided her time and hoped that Bolt would secure the security expert's job so he could work in the office alongside her. Although she knew he was always close by, she looked forward to him being able to roam freely through the offices. She'd set up the meeting between Hathaway and Bolt for midafternoon. And with so much riding on the outcome, as the interview hour approached, her nerves drew taut. It didn't help that she'd barely slept the night before.

In a very short time, she'd learned to rely on Bolt to protect her. Early this morning, when he'd watched her back while she'd spoken to Melanie, she'd felt safer due to his presence. Sure, the closer he could remain, the quicker he could intervene with any nefarious plans Hathaway might have. Just the memory of Hathaway's penetrating gaze on her made her antsy. Knowing he was in his office, and could call her in any time he desired, had her on edge. And yet, relying on Bolt, knowing he'd protect her, made her realize that sharing the danger was creating a heightened sense of trust between them.

Hathaway was up to something. Every instinct warned her that he was scheming to have her. She'd seen the predatory hunger in his eyes and understood that a man like Hathaway was unaccustomed to anyone defying his wishes.

Exactly one hour before Bolt was to arrive, Hathaway requested she come to his office. Her stomach knotted with dread. Sixty minutes could be a very long time to resist the man if he tuned his electric magnetism to high voltage. In his presence, she wished she could close her eyes, plug her ears and hold her breath to resist whatever he did to engage the erotic center of her brain.

But she had no idea how his powers worked. She only knew that at his summons both trepidation and anticipation filled her, and that her abnormal excitement and adrenaline rush was a telltale signal that he was already beginning to affect her.

Damn.

Stalling, she fixed coffee for Hathaway but none for herself. Despite walking slowly, she managed to delay only a few minutes before entering his office. She expected to find him behind his desk, but he stood at the window, surveying the city street below as if it were his private domain.

"We need to discuss last night." When he turned to

her, his stance reminded her of a predatory cat about to pounce.

Before she dropped the coffee cup, she set it on his desk. While she suspected he was referring to the electronic bug she'd found, his words had been ambiguous and could just as easily be regarding her orgasm. Unwilling to comment until she was certain of the subject, she remained silent, barely refraining from twisting her fingers together.

"You were most helpful." His tone was curt, thoughtful and not the least bit kind. His glinting eyes reminded her of diamonds, powerful and cutting.

"As executive assistant, it's my job to help you."

"Good. Then help me out, again."

His hard eyes pinned her and her nerve endings fired. All of them. It was if he'd waved an invisible magic wand and showered her in lust. Her body instantly turned on, and with pulse-pounding certainty, she knew he was determined to have her. Right here in his office. Right now.

Bolt's coming.

But not for an hour.

Get a grip.

How?

Focus on business.

"When Bob Timmins arrives, he'll sweep your office for other electronic devices. He'll also test your phone system and computers. He suggested doing so here in the office, in your limo and in your home."

Hathaway nodded and steepled his fingers under his

chin. "I usually prefer to work with women. I find them much more amenable and willing to follow orders."

Again, he drenched her with lust. Only the idea of "Bob Timmins" showing up for the interview and finding her naked with Hathaway kept her from ripping off her clothes.

She licked her bottom lip. "My former employer was very satisfied—"

"With you?"

"With Mr. Timmins," she corrected, continuing to play dumb although she knew damn well that Hathaway was toying with her. But he couldn't possibly know that her breasts ached and her nipples were hard. He couldn't know that her panties were damp. He couldn't know that, when she placed her hand into her jacket pocket and deliberately poked her finger with a thumb tack, the pain barely registered.

"So tell me, Amanda. How do you like working for me?"

She didn't want to answer personal questions, yet she had to take care not to offend him. If he fired her, she'd never get the proof she sought. Amanda took a deep breath, cocked her head to one side and appeared to be thinking about his question. Every second she stalled was another moment closer to Bolt's ETA and she would no longer be alone with Hathaway. "I haven't been here long enough to come to any conclusions."

"Come on. Are you telling me that I haven't made an impression on a bright girl like you?"

"Oh, you've made an impression. The office is beautiful—"

"I'm not asking about the decor."

"And your models are—"

"I'm not asking about the models, either."

If his powers were a storm, the wind would have been gale force. She'd been standing but her legs shook so badly, she feared her knees could no longer support her. She sank into a chair, but now she had to tilt her head back to look at Hathaway and his eyes glittered, revealing that he knew exactly what he was doing to her. And she hated how difficult it was to resist lusting after him when she despised him.

"Amanda, I'm asking if you like working with me."

"Oh. It's been…" She couldn't finish. She hated the man and he was turning her on. Oh, God. She was drawn so taut she thought she might explode for real even without Bolt's touch. Her mind was reeling from Hathaway's assault and she needed every working brain cell to resist, but Hathaway was playing word games, forcing her to split her concentration.

Gritting her teeth, she focused. She needed to come up with an inoffensive response.

"You were saying?" Hathaway prodded.

"Working for you…is interesting."

She couldn't carry on an intelligent conversation much longer. Not when she was having trouble keeping from panting. Not when she was barely controlling the urge to beg. She glanced at her watch and only five minutes had gone by. She wasn't going to hold out for an hour.

The thumb tack wasn't working as she'd hoped. She had the feeling if she tried to flee the office, Hathaway would stop her. And if he touched her, she might give in to the need burning through her like a wildfire.

She was losing control. She needed Bolt. Reaching into her pocket, she pressed the panic button. And prayed like hell that Bolt was only one floor below and would get here fast.

"Interesting." Hathaway drummed his fingers on his desk as he loomed over her. "*Interesting* is rather a bland word. Surely you can do better?"

"I'm not a walking thesaurus," she snapped, totally annoyed that he wanted her to think. She wasn't in the mood for mind games. No, she'd much rather…

No.

Yes. She'd much rather unknot Hathaway's tie, rip open his shirt.

He's the enemy.

I want him. God, help her, she did. Every cell in her body quivered. Her heart raced. She didn't understand how he could make her so insane for sex.

Bolt's coming. Wait. Wait. Wait.

Amanda was tearing apart. Her soul shouted *no.* But her body had needs of its own.

Bolt had promised he'd be here for her. Where the hell was he?

She was standing, walking toward Hathaway and not even the man's triumphant smile stopped her. And then outside Hathaway's office, she heard a commotion. Loud voices.

Bolt's voice.

He was here. And knowing help was seconds away strengthened her resolve. She changed direction and instead of heading toward Hathaway, she strode by him to the window. But she didn't see what was outside.

Her heart was racing. As much as she wanted to redirect her passion from Hathaway to Bolt, she simply couldn't fling herself into Bolt's arms the moment he came through that door or she'd give away their plan. She needed to leave the office, but didn't have a ready excuse. And thinking was so damn hard.

Bolt strode through the doors with Hathaway's secretary on his heels. "Sir, I'm sorry. I told him his appointment wasn't for an hour."

"Nonsense." Bolt looked at his watch. "Actually I'm ten minutes late and not a moment too soon."

Hathaway frowned. "Your conduct—"

"Silence." Bolt opened his briefcase and removed equipment, which was already beeping. "Not another word." He then proceeded to find bugs in Hathaway's phone, behind the light switch, in a desk drawer, under the carpet and even one on the back of the computer. By the time Bolt tossed the bugs into Hathaway's coffee, Hathaway's former anger seemed to have evaporated.

She could see Hathaway was impressed. He was going to hire "Bob Timmins" and that meant her cover wasn't blown. And luckily for her, Hathaway's attention had shifted, causing his animal magnetism to disappear. While she no longer had to deal with his continuing sensual assault, the aftereffects would take some time to settle. Her body didn't turn on and off like Bolt's electronic equipment, but slowly, she became more aware of her surroundings and how brilliantly Bolt had dealt with Hathaway.

The agent was accustomed to others kowtowing to his every wish. When Bolt had openly defied him, rudely barging into the office, Hathaway's astonishment had made his protests ineffective. Now Bolt had proven his usefulness and Hathaway's frown of outrage had turned to a frown of worry.

"You can talk now." Bolt put away his equipment and snapped shut his briefcase. He held out his hand. "Bob Timmins. Sorry to be so abrupt, but I didn't want to warn whomever was listening that I'm working with you."

"I don't believe I've hired you, Mr. Timmins."

"Ah, no problem." Bolt turned as if to leave. "If you don't want the best—"

"You're very cocky."

Bolt half turned. "I'm stating the truth. I can keep your conversations clean of eavesdroppers—unless they're Federal." Bolt faced him directly. "I don't take cases against the government."

"The government has no interest in me." Hathaway gestured to a chair as he sat behind his desk. "Please have a seat."

Amanda edged toward the door. She needed to wash her face, collect her thoughts. Regroup.

"Amanda, stay."

She leaned against the wall, putting as much distance between herself and Hathaway as possible. She resented the way he'd ordered her like a dog, but was powerless to do anything but obey. She also wished she was in a better state to help Bolt, but he seemed to be doing just fine on his own.

Hathaway respected bold moves and strength, and he recognized those traits in Bolt. But clearly he was also wary.

"You have references?" Hathaway demanded.

Bolt shook his head. "My clients prefer to remain anonymous—just as you will after I've solved your problem. I'll need keys to this building as well as your personal residence and vehicle. I'll also need computer passwords and alarm codes. If you are uncomfortable with that, then I suggest you hire someone else."

"We haven't discussed your fee." Hathaway leaned back in his chair and locked his fingers behind his head.

Bolt shrugged. "I can't quote a price until I see how big a problem you have. But from what I've seen so far, my services are going to be expensive."

"And why is that?" Hathaway challenged him.

"Because those aren't your garden-variety bugs. They are exorbitant in price and most equipment wouldn't have detected them. That might be why your regular sweeps missed them."

Hathaway didn't reveal that he believed his former security people betrayed him. Now that her lust had begun to subside, it seemed to Amanda that Hathaway liked to toy with everyone. He pushed, he tested, he tried to see what made a person tick by probing until he got a reaction that exposed real emotion. His tactic wasn't working with Bolt. But Hathaway didn't acknowledge that he was up against a better negotiator.

Instead his eyes flicked to Amanda for the first time since Bolt had entered the room. "You think I should hire him?"

"It's your decision."

"Of course it's my decision." He unlocked his hands from behind his head. "You can vouch that he does good work?"

She forced herself to respond to Hathaway and ignore Bolt as if the outcome was of no concern to her. "My former employer was satisfied, but I wasn't privy to all the details."

"That's not exactly what I call a full-scale endorsement." Hathaway's gaze returned to Bolt. "I prefer working with women."

Bolt grinned an easy smile of understanding. "I prefer doing everything with women."

"If you so much as talk to one of my models, you're fired."

"Not a problem." Bolt gazed straight at Hathaway. "I'm seeing someone right now."

Me. Me. Bolt was seeing Amanda, and Hathaway should keep his lust vibes to himself. She didn't want them. She certainly didn't want Hathaway. Compressing her lips, she didn't make a sound, but as if the strength of her hatred echoed through the office, Hathaway's gaze found Amanda again.

"You think if he's seeing someone it's enough to

keep him from going after some of the hottest women on the planet?"

"I don't know Mr. Timmins well enough to make that call." She didn't care if she sounded like a prim Sunday school teacher. The personal nature of the conversation was inappropriate and irritated her. But she knew some men were capable of committing to one woman. Her parents had had a great relationship and to the day they died together her father had adored her mother.

Hathaway stood, signaling the end of the interview. "If you want something, you ask Amanda. She'll get you everything you need."

"Understood. I'll also need a copy of your schedule."

"Why?"

"So I can stay out of your way as much as possible. With Amanda's help, I shouldn't have to bother you again."

The men shook hands, and Amanda prayed she could leave with Bolt, who'd opened the door to escort her out. Amanda desperately wanted a shower. She needed to wash her skin clean of Hathaway's games. The combination of staying on her toes mentally while he bombarded her with lusty emotions took a toll. She felt as though she'd just waged a battle.

But Hathaway's gaze went to her. "If you'll excuse us, Mr. Timmins. I need a private word with Amanda."

"I'll wait out there." Bolt didn't so much as glance her way. Calmly, he strode out of the office and closed the door, leaving her alone with Hathaway.

Once more she attempted to remain calm, but with

his renewed focus on her, his energy returned. Once again, he showered her in a drenching downpour of emotions she didn't want and tried to resist. "Yes, sir?"

"While Timmins is working for me, don't let him out of your sight."

She nodded, relief filling her that she was actually being ordered to stay with Bolt. Which would lessen her chances of being alone with Hathaway. The tension seemed worse when they were one on one. Perhaps he focused more on her. Perhaps she couldn't distract herself as easily without Bolt there. Either way, she felt compelled to take a step toward Hathaway and only the utmost concentration on remaining still kept her rooted. And she clung to the notion that once she left here, she would be with Bolt, always with Bolt.

Hathaway's next words burst her bubble of hope. "However, I'll expect Bolt to cool his heels in reception while you report to me at least once a day."

AFTER HATHAWAY'S COMMENT, Amanda fled to the rest room. As if sensing she was barely in control of herself, Bolt had whispered for her to take all the time she needed. She gulped in oxygen and steadied herself on the counter. Leaning over the sink, Amanda splashed cool water on her face, determined to wash away her wild expression. With her pupils dilated, her face flushed, her hands shaking, she looked far from the calm executive assistant she was supposed to be.

When one of Hathaway's models exited a stall, Amanda almost didn't recognize the leggy *Vogue* cover model from Hathaway's party. Frances had changed her hair from blond to cinnamon-auburn, and without makeup, she didn't appear nearly as haughty as she had the night of Hathaway's party.

Plunking a designer bag on the counter, Frances leaned forward toward the mirror to examine her flawless complexion. But her arrogant gaze rested on Amanda. "There's no use fighting the compulsion."

"Excuse me?" Startled that the famous model had actually spoken to her, Amanda blotted her face dry with a paper towel and reminded herself to turn the conversation toward Melanie if she could. Yet, she thought it ironic that of all times, Frances had chosen to speak to her now when she was still hampered by the aftereffects of her meeting with Hathaway.

"You're fighting yourself." Frances spoke as if to an idiot, her tone condescending.

"I am?" Amanda played dumb, hoping to draw more information from her. Frances had been around Hathaway's organization a while and had to know quite a bit about his agency.

"Better women than you have tried and failed to resist Hathaway." Frances opened her makeup bag and applied cream to her eye lids, face and neck in swift professional strokes.

"Really?"

"Sure. People assume models are just a pretty face, with no brain. Some of us have a life beyond our careers, you know." Frances shook her head and her glorious hair shimmered under the florescent lights. She fluffed it to perfection then spritzed on a liquid scented with jasmine. "I'm taking business classes at night and learning to invest my own money, so I needn't depend on managers. A model's career is short and too many managers are crooks. I work too hard to leave my assets to someone else's management."

Amanda nodded in admiration. "At least when you're done, you won't be dependent on Hathaway like Melanie Carter." She threw the name of Donna's friend out there in hopes Frances would keep chatting.

"Melanie's old news. Hathaway moved on a long time ago."

"So they were an item?"

"Not after the accident."

"You think Melanie still has feelings for Hathaway?" Amanda pushed a little more.

Frances shrugged, but didn't frown. The supermodel likely had too much Botox to move her facial muscles. "Melanie wanted a wedding ring. Hathaway wanted Donna."

"Donna?" Had her sister come between Hathaway and Melanie? Amanda pretended ignorance. "I don't believe I've met her."

"She's dead. Took a bullet to her head and her body ended up in a Dumpster. Nasty business. Hathaway took her death real hard."

Now this was interesting. Donna had told her sister about her feelings for Hathaway but Amanda hadn't known Hathaway had returned those feelings. Perhaps Amanda's initial suspicion about the superagent was off target and Hathaway had nothing to do with her sister's death. And it now seemed Melanie had motive to kill since it appeared Donna had stolen Hathaway's affections. But if Melanie had killed Donna, why would she have contacted Amanda? Had telling her about the stalker and the diary been red herrings? And if Melanie wanted to get back in Hathaway's good graces, would she tell Hathaway that Amanda was Donna's sister?

Or was Melanie exactly what she seemed? A friend of Donna's who didn't know enough to go to the police but still wanted to help. And why should she come forward when Hathaway was supporting her? Unless her conscience was nagging her?

Amanda simply didn't have enough facts to judge Melanie's true motives. Digging for more information, she tried to keep her tone casual. "With the way Hathaway flirts, I wouldn't have guessed he was hurting too badly."

Frances waved a lipstick tube at her. "Oh, don't get me wrong, Hathaway is never loyal to anyone. But Donna was certainly one of his favorites."

"She must have been very beautiful." Amanda tried not to sound too interested.

Frances tossed aside the lipstick and applied blush to her high cheekbones. "He was more preoccupied with her brains. She used to be a chemist." Frances spit out the word chemist as if instead Donna had been a whore instead of a world-renowned expert.

"Is Hathaway interested in chemistry?"

"Oh, yeah." Frances chuckled without smiling. "He's

very interested in the chemistry between a man and his women."

Amanda shrugged, glad that Bolt still had his receiver and was listening to the conversation, too. She looked forward to hearing his assessment of Frances's words, and more importantly, he would understand what was keeping Amanda in the bathroom so long. "I don't understand."

"Hathaway wanted Donna to use her expertise to create the ultimate aphrodisiac perfume. She wanted to model. So they compromised."

So that was why Hathaway had held back on getting her assignments. He wanted her working on the perfume. "Did she finish the project before she—"

"I don't know. If she did finish, Hathaway's obviously keeping it all to himself." Frances dabbed a drop of perfume between her breasts. "Hathaway once took me to his bedroom. He had a perfume bottle sitting out on his dresser. When I started to pick up the bottle to try to sniff, he went postal on me, kicked me out of his room and told me I'd be lucky if I ever worked again."

"You seem to be doing fine."

Frances smiled, but her eyes remained cool and arrogant. "Oh, we made up. He even apologized. And let me tell you, Hathaway does everything in grand style. He flew me on his private jet to Tahiti."

"Just the two of you?"

"I am beautiful, am I not?" Frances must have thought the question rhetorical. She didn't wait for a response and kept chatting. "This was shortly after

Donna died and there were enough rumors flying around. He couldn't afford to have his top-earning model leave for another agency. So he bought me the finest champagne and caviar, brought me to an exclusive island and spent hours making love to me. He was actually almost sweet…" she began, and then her eyes hardened.

"What?"

"Once we returned, he changed. I'm not the possessive type but Frances does not stand in line, if you know what I mean."

"I sure do," she agreed and refrained from wincing. Amanda detested when people referred to themselves as if they were royalty.

Frances snapped shut her compact and dropped it into her bag. "But Hathaway's not going after me. He's focusing on you. It's easiest to enjoy him while his interest lasts, then simply let him move on. My advice is not to fight him."

"Did he tell you to say that?" Amanda asked.

Frances's eyes widened. "As a matter of fact, he did."

HATHAWAY DRUMMED his fingers on his desk. Right about now, Frances ought to be giving Amanda his message. Although he couldn't trust Frances not to gossip and put her own twist on their past, she would do as she was told. She wouldn't risk losing her contracts.

Since Hathaway had found intimidation and fear helped the bottle do its work, he'd suggested to Frances that she should tell Amanda just enough to make her think Hathaway was dangerous. Some women liked that edge in a man. They found the danger exciting.

Either a frightened Amanda or a turned-on Amanda would work in his favor. And he would see to it that she spent more time in his presence so he could practice his powers on her. It wasn't that he found her so attractive, but that he didn't understand how she was resisting him. And if one woman could resist him, then others could, too.

Being all powerful had too many advantages for him to ignore the significance of Amanda's immunity. To counter her strength, he needed to know exactly how she was doing so.

And one way or another he would find out.

9

BOLT HATED HOW Hathaway was trying to manipulate Amanda. After listening to her conversation with Frances, it was clear the man had manipulated Frances and Melanie, too. While it remained unclear whether the woman cooperated voluntarily or not, he ached to take Amanda into his arms and comfort her, but there were too many prying eyes around the office. So when she exited the rest room, looking much more together than when she'd entered, he gestured toward the elevator. "Since I promised to stay out of Hathaway's hair, let's start at his personal residence."

"We'll need to stop at his secretary's desk for—"

He held up keys. "Per Hathaway's instructions, she also gave me the security code. If you're ready, we're set to go."

They didn't have to go outside. Hathaway's agency was on the top floor of the offices in the building and his suite was just one story up on the first level of private condominiums. If Hathaway had to be in close proximity to the perfume bottle for him to tap into the special powers, he had that neatly covered without having to move the bottle.

Bolt and Amanda couldn't speak privately in the crowded elevator, and he had to wait until he'd unlocked the door and turned off the alarm to Hathaway's suite to take her into his arms. The suite looked exactly as it did on the monitor, spacious, luxurious and decorated in the height of New York hip fashion. Today the Shey Group had made sure the maid had car trouble and wouldn't be in until tomorrow and the chef had the night off due to Hathaway's dinner plans; he was to be a keynote dinner speaker for a business association. He then planned to take in a Broadway show. They had the place to themselves and wouldn't be interrupted.

And finally he could say the words at the forefront of his mind. "When you hit the panic button, I got there as soon as I could."

"It seemed like forever." At the memory, her irises darkened. "To resist him, I kept thinking about you."

"Did that work?"

"A little. But it had been too long since we were together and I was weakening," she admitted, molding her body to his and smoothing her hands over his shoulders and neck.

He needed to make love to her. But now that they were in Hathaway's suite, he also had to grab this chance to search for the perfume bottle and the diary. He was willing to let her prioritize the tasks. "What do you want to do first?"

"There's no way I can return to Hathaway unless we—"

"Agreed."

He started to kiss her, but she turned her head slightly so instead of finding her mouth, his lips landed on her cheek. He would take what he could get. He trailed a hot kiss over her cheek to her ear, caught her lobe between his teeth and nibbled as he inhaled her scent.

She giggled. "That tickles."

"Mmm."

"You're distracting me."

"Isn't that what you wanted?"

"Yes and no."

He nibbled her collarbone. "You're contradicting yourself."

"Am I?" She wrinkled her nose. "I'm not complaining about our former lovemaking, but, perhaps this time…"

"This time?" He licked her neck.

She shivered. "I can't think when you do that."

"Thinking isn't required."

"Maybe it is."

He straightened and ignored the tension in his groin, the swell of his balls, the urge to have her right here, right now. Obviously she was trying to tell him something important, and he wanted to hear what she was thinking. Only he wanted to make love to her more. Yet, he put her concerns first—which only reinforced in his own mind how much he was coming to care about her.

He drew a deep draught of air into his lungs and released it slowly. "All right. I'm listening."

"Every time you've satisfied me, we've made love hard and fast."

"And?"

"I'm not complaining. I was desperate and needed exactly what you gave me."

He suddenly understood exactly where she was going. "So, if we prolonged and drew out the lovemaking, maybe you'd be less susceptible to Hathaway."

He hoped she'd been hinting that she wanted something besides a physical release, that she wanted her emotions involved, too. But now wasn't the time to ask. He didn't want to push her too hard before she was ready. Obviously his feelings for her were way ahead of hers for him. Yes, she'd accepted the need for sexual intimacy between them. But now he was suggesting raising the stakes to another level.

"Sounds like a plan," she agreed.

And he couldn't have approved more. If she was sexually satisfied and emotionally fortified against Hathaway, she might find resisting his powers much easier.

Not only did the idea make sense, he wondered why he hadn't thought of it sooner. Probably because he had a lot on his mind. While he couldn't help but admire her straightforward attitude and willingness to adapt to the circumstances, he also wondered what she was feeling. When she wasn't sexy and saucy and sassy with the need to make love, she was self-contained. She talked less about herself than any woman he'd ever known. At first, he'd been attracted to her confidence and her adaptability, but now he wanted to go deeper, learn more about her.

He kissed her on the mouth this time, his arms around her, his mouth angling over hers. They fused lip-to-lip, chest to chest, pelvis to pelvis, and he could feel her heart beating at a quick tempo, her nipples hardening.

Physically she appeared to want him as much as he wanted her. But he wanted to take his time making love to her, wanted to savor what it felt like to be inside her. And although the testosterone coursing through him might be demanding he hurry, he was not about to allow his hormones to get in the way of her request to go slowly. Prolonged and easy was the order of the day.

Her kiss tasted of anticipation, eagerness and pure feminine heat and he savored holding her and keeping her safe as much as he looked forward to assuaging both their needs. He slid his hands to her waist, under her blouse, and the warmth of her bare back under his fingertips was sheer heaven. He loved stroking her silky skin, adored the way the friction set off a matching thrum of electricity that went straight to his core.

"Mmm. You feel good," he whispered into her mouth.

"You'd feel better if we weren't wearing any clothes."

"You are the one who said we needed to slow down." He smiled at her, knowing that if they did as she suggested and removed all their clothing, holding back would be almost impossible. "I'm taking off one item of your clothing and I get to decide which one."

She pulled back, blinked, clearly startled, then she laughed, her tone low and husky, her eyes glimmering with excitement. "Okay. As long as I get to do the same for you."

He didn't have to consider which item of clothing to remove for very long. He trailed his fingers up her back and unhooked her bra. Then ever so slowly, he worked the lacy fabric out from beneath her blouse. He took his time, and along the way, he managed to graze the underside of her breasts, trace the inner curves and brush her nipples with the back of his hand. And she didn't even pretend to hold still. She let out soft sighs of encouragement and wriggled to enhance the contact.

And when he finally drew the bra out of her sleeve, she was trembling, yet eyeing him in speculation. She loosened his tie and he thought she meant to remove it. But she simply flipped the tie aside so she could unbutton his shirt.

Taking her time, fingers shaking, she unfastened his top button ever so slowly and fingered his skin beneath, allowing the cool air to play over his flesh. He figured she'd move on to the second button next. But instead, she dipped her hands into the waistband of his slacks.

He sucked in his breath, immediately going granite hard. "You don't play fair."

"Where's the fun in that?" She pulled at the edge of his shirt, and he realized that going slowly might be the most difficult task he'd ever set himself.

Her fingers teased and taunted. Featherlight, her caresses had his nerves leaping and his breath ragged, but it was his heart that she touched. And he suddenly had the desire to whisk her away from Hathaway's suite to a place where their need for one another would be all their own, a place where work wouldn't influence their passion for one another.

Obligation stopped him from making the suggestion. Obligation to Kincaid and the Shey Group. Their organization maintained a platinum reputation because their agents never quit an operation. And even if he could bring himself to do so, Amanda wouldn't rest until her sister's killer was behind bars. That she'd been willing to go so far, that she was willing to put up with Hathaway, told him, more than any words could, just how determined she was.

And although he admired that determination, a part of him, the selfish part, wanted her to make love to him for himself, not to satiate a need created by Hathaway. Although he knew deep down that Amanda wouldn't make love to him unless she already liked him, Bolt realized he wanted more than that.

When she peeled off his shirt, sweat beaded on his brow. Since their relationship was no longer just about sex—at least, for him—he decided taking some risk was in order. Peeling off clothing was no longer enough. He wanted to peel back her veneer and learn what was hiding beneath.

"You're so serious. Are you having second thoughts?" she murmured, leaning in to lick his nipple.

"My thoughts are about getting inside your head."

"And here I thought you wanted to get under my skirt." She leaned back and stared at him.

"I want that, too," he admitted. "I'm not willing to settle for half measures. I want all of you."

Her eyebrows drew together and her irises glazed with a puzzled look. "You aren't talking about making love, are you?"

"I don't know much about you."

"You've read my file."

"I don't know your favorite food."

"Scrambled eggs."

"Or if you think it's more romantic to gaze at the stars or the ocean."

"Actually I like to look at you and you still have too many clothes on. Are we going to search for the bottle or make love?"

"Both." Despite her wish to go slowly, he could see her impatience building, the tension making her lower lip quiver as she fought for control.

And in truth, now was not the time for a soul-baring conversation. He took her hand and headed through the living room. "Come on. Let's search for that diary and the perfume bottle."

"Where are we going?"

"To his bedroom."

He led her down a wide hallway with a marble floor and an Oriental carpet runner, past contemporary paintings of artists he didn't recognize and sculptures of men and women in various tasteful embraces, backlit by carefully placed lighting. The decor screamed expensive.

Double doors of burnished cherry opened into a private library that doubled as an office off the master suite. Here the paintings and sculptures became more erotic. Since his surveillance hadn't penetrated this deep into Hathaway's private room, Bolt slowed his steps and took stock.

"Hathaway could have installed a safe behind any of those books or paintings."

Amanda frowned at the floor-to-ceiling shelves. "It'll take hours to search behind all those books."

"Let's try the master bedroom, first." He tugged Amanda back into his arms. "But first, it's time to remove another item of clothing."

"I was hoping you'd say that." She tugged off his tie, which he felt silly wearing since he was shirtless. "This time, I go first. And the tie doesn't count."

"Whatever." His attempt to appear casual didn't come off as he intended. But remaining unaffected was impossible as she unzipped his slacks. And of course, she took her time, tugging them down and over his hips, normally an easy task. But his erection tented his boxers and she seemed to take great pleasure in running her fingers over the cotton.

He kicked off his shoes and stepped out of his pants, then peered at her as if trying to decide what item of her clothing to remove next. The idea of her topless pleased him, but he didn't want to be predictable. Kneeling, he slid his hands up her thighs, skipped over the gun at her thigh and found the triangle of silk between her legs already damp.

"I like the idea of you searching the apartment without wearing anything beneath your clothes."

At his statement, she bit her bottom lip. "I was certain you'd go for my blouse."

"That would be fantastic but since you're going to be searching under Hathaway's bed—"

She broke into an adorable chuckle. "On my hands and knees?"

"Oh, yeah." That image literally made his mouth water and he rubbed his hands together like the greedy man he was for the sight of her.

"Why, you'll be able to look right up my skirt. But you wouldn't think of peeking, would you?" she asked, clearly egging him on.

He grinned. "I'm not going to peek."

"You aren't?" She sounded disappointed.

And he hated to disappoint a lady. "I'm going to stare."

She didn't blush. She simply wriggled her hips, urging him to hurry and remove her panties. And as much as he wanted to rush, he remembered her words—even if she didn't. So he took his sweet time, taking every opportunity to stroke and caress, until bit by bit, he ever so slowly removed them.

"Just knowing that you aren't wearing anything under that skirt is intoxicating."

"Maybe I'll give up wearing panties on a permanent basis then."

Whatever she meant, she'd raised his hopes. "I like the sound of that."

"I think we should search Hathaway's room now."

She sauntered ahead of him, exaggerating the sway of her hips as if to remind him he'd removed her panties. But he didn't need any reminders. Sheesh. Thinking about her bare under her skirt had him fantasizing all kinds of scenarios, and he followed in a daze.

But she wasn't as in control as she pretended, either. Not when her moisture had beaded onto his fingers.

Not when her nipples were so tight and pebbled that they poked through her blouse, inviting his touch like a welcome sign.

She wanted him. He wanted her. But life wasn't that simple. They had a job to do and, while he fully intended to satisfy them both, their relationship was growing more complex by the moment.

He'd never met a woman quite like her. She might have been a little reluctant to give herself over to him at first. But she'd thrown herself into the role so wholeheartedly, he had to wonder if she'd been holding back her entire life. He liked to think she'd been waiting for him.

But weighing on him was the possibility that when the mission was over, they might not see one another again. However, Bolt was a man more suited to action than dwelling on what might be.

He entered the bedroom and skidded to a halt, all thoughts vanishing in the face of the incredible sight before him. Amanda was on her hands and knees, her bottom high in the air as she searched under the bed. With her skirt hiked up her thighs, she presented him with a most enticing view. Coming closer, his heart thudded. He ached to thrust into her without warning.

But he wouldn't. And she knew he wouldn't. She'd deliberately assumed her pose to taunt him and it was surely working. He felt ready to explode and his exasperation and yearning hardened his tone. "You're incorrigible."

"Thanks. I'll take that as a compliment." She wriggled farther under the bed, her voice muffled. "Would you happen to have a flashlight?"

He forced his gaze from the delectable pink flesh peeking out from between her buttocks and searched the room, his chest tight, his fingers burning to touch her. The bureau's top was bare and so was the nightstand, except for the clock radio and a lamp. Bolt picked up the lamp, kneeled and angled it under the bed, giving both of them a clearer view.

"That's better," she murmured.

"What's under there?"

"Books. Magazines. Old mail. Likely everything he wants to hide from the maid." She began to wriggle back out, papers crinkling in her hand.

Bolt reached under her skirt, placed his palm flat over her bottom and lips. "You sure you haven't missed anything?"

She arched into him. "I could look again."

He slipped one finger into her and placed another right on her clit, then tapped her there.

"Oh." She shimmied. "I thought we… What about searching… Damn, I can't think when you…"

He loved distracting her. He adored stoking her. Best of all he liked how she took an outrageous idea and followed through with it. He'd merely suggested that he'd wanted her in this position and she'd acted as if there was no place she'd rather be, no one she'd rather be with.

"You really have a lovely bottom." He stroked and petted and teased while she squirmed and wriggled in a most enticing fashion that made her rounded flesh quiver.

Leaning forward, he bit her cheek where it arched so sweetly under his palm.

"Ow."

With a long slow graze of his tongue, he licked away her pain. "Was that a complaint?"

"Yes. No. I don't know-w-w." Her words ended on a squeal as he nipped her other cheek.

Again he licked away the nip of pain. "You sound confused."

"That's because…you…you are…making me…crazy."

He increased the friction on her clit, rubbing quicker, pleased she was so damp, so slick, so ready for more. "Crazy in a good way?"

"Mmm."

"You're sure?"

"Yes. Yes. Yes."

She was tensing, so close to bursting. And remembering she'd asked him to go slowly, he stopped and drew her out from under the bed, and then tried to pull her close.

Tossing her hair out of her eyes, she twisted to glare at him. Eyes glazed, mouth pouting, she looked frazzled and sexy. "What are you doing? Why are we stopping?"

"Don't you want to read Hathaway's mail?"

Her eyes widened then narrowed. "You're toying with me."

"Yeah." He grinned at her obvious frustration, picked up half the pile of mail and shoved it toward her.

"You." She ignored the mail. "You are so in trouble."

"Really?"

"Oh, yeah." She yanked down his shorts before he'd realized what she was about. "Two can play this game."

"So you think you can hold out longer than me?" He laughed at her aggression, thoroughly enjoying her combination of pouting and threatening and brazen confidence.

"Of course, I can hold out longer than you." Her tone was breathless and haughty. She grabbed his sex with a look of mischief in her eyes, a cocky tilt of her head and salty challenge in her tone. "Go ahead. Start reading. Don't let little old me distract you."

She'd never looked more beautiful than she did right then. With her hair wild, her chin smudged with dust from under the bed and green sparks in her eyes, she looked like the woman of his dreams, dreams he hadn't even known he'd had until now. She might have been challenging him, but he didn't care who gave in first, because in the end they would both win, they would both give and receive pleasure and they'd both get satisfaction.

But the longer he could hold out, the longer they could play, and he so enjoyed playing her. How could he not? He liked everything about her. Her feminine scent mixed with her citrus soap. The firm texture of her skin. The way, when he squeezed her bottom, the firm flesh plumped into his hand. But most of all her spirit complemented the fire in his.

She was three parts sugar, one part spice, and he never knew which part she would offer up. He only knew that he was fast becoming addicted.

Already she was learning what pleased him. A careful lover, she'd discovered where he was most sensitive and used the knowledge to advantage. And it wasn't long before she had him gasping, sweating, holding back with every cell of his being. Because he would not give in to her caresses. This time he was determined they would climax together.

So he let her splay her hands over him, and when he could take not a second more, when he was about to erupt, when he was about to yank away, she sensed the moment. And she stopped, leaving him on the brink.

Chest heaving, groin burning for release, he had to clench the mattress to prevent himself from grabbing her, sinking his sex into her heat and taking her to where they both wanted to go. And when he finally regained a measure of calm, he found her watching him with a satisfied grin.

"You don't look so in control right now," she teased as she stood and began opening and closing drawers. "You did say you were going to help me search the room, didn't you?"

The only thing he wanted to search right now was every inch of her body. And his physical reaction to her, his balls, tight and full, made standing painful. And while he'd never wanted anything in his life as much as he wanted her at this moment, he wasn't about to give in. So he took several deep breaths and checked out the room to distract himself from the amazing Amanda Lane.

The California King didn't even take up one quarter of the large bedroom. From his position next to the bed, Bolt glimpsed a master bathroom to the right and a walk-in closet to the left. If he was going to hide a wall safe, he'd choose the closet. With a myriad of clothing, sporting equipment and shoes hanging from an assortment of fixtures, it would be relatively easy to conceal a safe.

Of course the perfume bottle might be right out in the open, but Bolt suspected Hathaway didn't trust his staff enough to leave such a valuable item within easy-grabbing range. Heading for the closet, he didn't miss Amanda's appreciative glance at his nudity.

While she still wore her blouse and skirt, he was naked, if he didn't count his socks. Shaking his head at how that had occurred, he grinned at his predicament, yet he didn't approach her. He needed time to cool down.

And then she shrieked in triumph. "Look what I found."

10

AMANDA HELD UP the shoe box she'd discovered in the top drawer of Hathaway's bureau. She'd opened the lid to discover half a dozen letters. The handwriting on the stationery looked familiar and Amanda's gaze dropped to the signature. "This one's from my sister."

"What's it say?"

After sitting on the bed, she read quickly and summarized aloud. "She thanked Hathaway for all he'd done for her and told him that modeling was much more exciting than being a chemist. She suggested that he follow her advice and send the bottle to a colleague who was discreet and who could analyze it. She claimed that without laboratory equipment, she couldn't do his project justice."

"What else is in there?"

"I wonder why Hathaway saved this letter." Amanda lifted the stationery and sniffed, hoping a scent that would hint of her sister might linger, but she sneezed.

"Bless you."

"Thanks. The unsmeared dust on the outside of the box suggests Hathaway hasn't opened it for a long time. But he saved Donna's letter. Why?"

Bolt leaned over her shoulder. "Maybe he wanted to keep the chemist's address."

"You think he sent the bottle to Dr. Kevin Lee?" she read the scientist's name and didn't recognize it.

"We'll check and find out. Was that the only letter from your sister?"

"Yes." She flipped through them quickly and another caught her eye. "Oh, my. This one's from Melanie and the other is from Frances—and both of them...are odd."

While she spoke, Bolt was searching behind paintings and draperies, knocking on the woodwork walls for hidden panels and opening more drawers. Yet, she had the impression he was listening intently to her and she appreciated that he trusted her to read the letters for clues without immediately taking over and demanding to read every word.

She read quickly and condensed the main points. "Melanie wants money. Frances's note is more threatening."

Bolt looked her way. "What do you mean by threatening? Blackmail? Death threats?"

"I'm not sure." She reread the pertinent parts out loud. "Melanie writes, 'I'm in so much pain. You have no idea how I miss our good times together. While I know we can never recapture what we once had, I hold you responsible for the accident and what I've suffered since. The least you can do is give me the money you owe me.'"

"That could be blackmail. But it's by no means enough to accuse her of anything. She didn't threaten him."

"But the note itself could imply a threat—we simply don't have enough information." She moved on to another letter. "Frances's note is even more vague, but it's in her usual arrogant tone. She says, 'I know what you did. Stay out of my way, or else.'"

"Or else what?"

"She doesn't say." Frustrated, Amanda's gaze sought out Bolt. He didn't seem the least perturbed that their data was incomplete—or that she'd interrupted their lovemaking. And since he wore his skin as comfortably as he wore his clothes, she couldn't help noting that while his mind might be on the mission, his interest in her hadn't abated.

"We'll have to find Melanie and speak to her as well as Frances and ask more questions."

"Their letters probably have nothing to do with Donna."

"But if they'll talk to us, we'll almost certainly learn more about how Hathaway operates. In addition, I'll check with your sister's expert to see if he ever examined the bottle. In the meantime, I suggest we keep searching. And…"

"And?" She carefully refolded the letters and replaced them in the shoe box before putting them back in the bureau where she'd found them.

"There's more to be done here than figuring out puzzles." The sparkle in his tone warned her to glance up, just as Bolt scooped her around the waist and tugged her back against his front, positioning her before Hathaway's full-length mirror. "It's time to remove another article of your clothing."

She laughed. "I was wondering if you'd forgotten about me."

He nudged her from behind. "Do I feel like I've forgotten anything?"

As he bent his head to nibble on a sensitive spot in the curve of her neck, he reached around to unbutton her blouse. Although their foreplay had stopped and started several times, her body had no difficulty picking up where they had left off. The delays had only served to combine anticipation, temptation and excitement until she was certain that if he added anything else to the mix she'd boil over.

"Watch." Tone curt and demanding, she tilted her chin, directing her gaze to the mirror.

First she took in the sight of him. One rakish lock of dark hair fell across his broad forehead, shadows accentuating the chiseled planes of his cheekbones that gave him a dangerous air.

Then the movement of his hands drew her attention. With her blouse unfastened, he parted the material enough to see the curves of her breasts. His tan hand splayed across her white midriff and the contrast reminded her of caramel and cream, sweet, luscious and distinctive. Although she knew the perfume bottle was influencing her, she liked the sight of him touching her. The way his powerful shoulders and chest dwarfed her made her feel cherished, alluring and wanted. And when his eyes gleamed with mischief, she suspected she was in for a playful and enticing evening.

In the mirror, her own reflection appeared wanton. Her short skirt, the open blouse, her lack of lingerie was as sexy as if she'd been bare. Maybe sexier. And when she attempted to shrug the blouse from her shoulders and free her breasts to his hands, he nipped her shoulder.

"Hold still for me as I did for you." His words were half request, half demanding and shot a thrill through her. She liked Bolt, enjoyed playing his games, which always ended in so much pleasure. And she enjoyed how he could switch roles with ease, a sign he was a man confident with his sexuality.

Still, she hesitated and checked the time on the alarm clock.

"Relax. Hathaway won't return for hours."

Amanda already knew enough about Hathaway to know that the man followed his schedule as if he were in the military. No way would he miss an opportunity to make a keynote speech. So she leaned her head back against Bolt's chest and watched him part her blouse inch by inch to finally reveal her breasts. Tiny goose bumps rose on her areolae, clamoring for attention, but Bolt ignored the pointy, aching nubs at their center. Instead he caressed her breasts, the outer and inner curves, underneath and above. He traced sensuous, circular paths over and around her sensitive flesh until she thought she'd go mad from his teasing.

And her face reflected her needs. Her heavy-lidded eyes, her pouty mouth, her chest rising and falling with each ragged breath, all revealed how much she was enjoying what he was doing to her. She caught the frenzied look in her eyes, the wild need to seek release.

Watching herself seemed to increase the sensation,

made their act seem more erotic, more over the top. She observed his lips tease her ear, the sensation doubly delicious as his breath fanned her earlobes and nape before his lips and tongue followed suit with long shivery caresses. Although she watched, his little nips still surprised her, teased her. And just when he had her focusing on her neck, he pinched her nipples, causing a hitch of electricity that zinged straight to her core.

She lowered her hands to her skirt to remove it, but he took her wrists and placed her hands over her head, behind his neck. The position arched her spine, raised her breasts and he cupped them, then used the pads of his fingertips to strum and pluck and pinch until she pumped her hips against him, determined that he place his sex inside her.

Gently he urged her to take a step forward, then another until her nipples touched the cool mirror and her breath fogged her reflection. Finally he unwound her hands from behind his neck and placed each palm on the mirror.

The combination of the cold glass against her front, mixed with the heat of him along her back, electrified her skin. Then he stepped away, but she didn't miss his heat. She was on fire, burning for him. She missed his touch, though. Needed it like a parched desert thirsted for a hard rain. Savoring the moment when fantasy and reality collided, the pleasure kept escalating along with her anticipation. She was about to demand that he return, but then heard foil ripping and realized what he was doing.

And then her capacity for realization vanished as he gently pulled back her hips and spread her legs as wide as the skirt allowed. Her forearms and palms rested on the mirror, which meant her breasts no longer touched the glass. However, with her spine arched and her bottom tilted upward due to the heels she still wore, he had easy access to all of her. But the skirt was making her insane. Because somehow she knew he wasn't going to take her fully until he removed it.

And he didn't seem inclined to do so.

He was too busy dipping his fingers between her thighs, his touch so light that she pumped her hips for more. However, he refused to take her hint, leaving behind and neglecting the damp moisture between her legs in favor of stroking her inner thighs and her bottom.

Her legs trembled, her breasts quivered. She needed him inside her so badly that she was shaking with the need. But he totally ignored her willingness to have him right now. And she now cursed herself for asking him to take his time. She hadn't expected him to delay this long. She hadn't known that extending the pleasure would be such torture.

And yet, she was determined to remain as still as he had for her. Because every stroke fed her fever to have more. She grated her bottom against his pelvis, vexed by the skirt that kept his flesh from entering her.

She squeezed her eyes shut. "In case you...hadn't noticed—"

"I'm noticing everything."

"—I'm ready for...you...ah...now."

"I'm noticing how your sweet moisture is coating my fingers. I'm noticing how plump and sensitive you are. How you respond so sweetly to every caress. How much you like when I do this." He flicked her clit lightly and she groaned. "And how much you like when I fondle the insides of your thighs. But this gun is in the way."

His voice was low and throaty and eager as he unfastened the holster's strap and placed the gun aside. Yet he still held back. She ground her teeth in frustration. He was so good at revving her up, then keeping her right on the brink of orgasm. She hadn't known she could take so much pleasure without bursting. But he noticed ever little quiver, read her as easily as if she'd handed him a damn manual. And his expertise had her close to begging.

She was about to turn around and grab him, when his fingers found her sweet spot. Sheesh. The man knew how to keep her going. Her entire world focused on his fingers, sliding, stroking.

Never ceasing his coaxing, he finally removed her skirt. And all she could think was for him to hurry, hurry, hurry. She arched her spine, raising her bottom, offering herself and finally she felt him insert the tip of his sex into her. And she slammed backward, ramming him home. She exploded and like a volcano bursting lava, she flowed red-hot with pleasure that went on and on and on.

Sometime during his frenzied loveplay, she understood that he wasn't done. His fingers beat a rhythm on her clit and she kept exploding like fireworks, one blast feeding the next. Incredible multiorgasms shocked her with their intensity. Her body becoming so sensitive that each caress shot another jolt through her, until she couldn't breathe. Or stand. Or think.

She had no idea when he found his own release. Because he never stopped moving or teasing her, not even after she screamed.

And every cell in her short-circuited from the torturous pleasure.

BOLT CAUGHT HER in his arms before she collapsed on the floor. Damn, she was lovely, beautiful in how she could give herself up to pleasure. He eased into a chair, settled her across his lap and waited in anticipation for her eyelids to open.

Even in a daze, with her skin flushed, a slight smile and her hair cascading over his arm, she gave him enjoyment. He liked bringing her to heights she'd never experienced before.

In his experience women liked to talk about their relationships, analyze the details, figure out where it was going. But Amanda was mysterious and remarkably self-contained. However, she made up for repressing her emotions by expressing herself through uninhibited sex.

As he watched her eyes flutter, then open to stare at him, he figured now might be as good a time as any to find out what was going on in that head of hers, especially before he got in any deeper. "Welcome back."

Wonder rounded her lovely eyes. "I didn't know I

could have so many orgasms that each one sparked the next. It was an incredible experience. Thank you."

He cuddled her closer to his chest and stroked her hair. "You sound as if you're thanking me for dinner."

She laughed in obvious delight. "Oh, sex with you is much better than dinner."

That wasn't the response he was looking for. She'd said *sex,* not lovemaking. But he couldn't judge her feelings on the significance of one or two words.

"I'm glad you enjoyed yourself."

She sighed and snuggled against him. "I most certainly did."

"And?"

"And what?" Her tone was lazy and totally relaxed.

He swallowed his hesitation. "What happens to *us* when the mission is over?"

"Us?"

"Us. You and me."

When she blinked at him and bit her bottom lip, he pressed her.

"Are we going to be together?" he asked.

"Do you want us to be?" Her eyes darkened into twin pools of murky sea-green, deep and swirling and impossible to navigate without capsizing.

The woman was unbelievable at turning his words back on him. And yet, he supposed she had as much right to ask him about his feelings as he did about hers. Still, extracting each word from her was as difficult as opening an oyster in search of pearls.

"I want to see more of you."

She laughed. "You've already seen all of me."

"I want us to spend time together."

"I'd like that."

She'd agreed so easily, barely considering his comment. But he had no idea if that meant her feelings ran so deep that she didn't have to stop and examine them, or that she simply wanted to keep doing what they were already doing.

"That's all you have to say?"

"You asked me if I wanted to spend time together after the mission. I answered in the affirmative. What more is there to say?"

He shook his head at her. Was she deliberately yanking his chain? Still fuzzy from the lovemaking? Or evading his questions and/or her own feelings? "I want to know if you want more from me than sex."

"I'd like to know the answer to that question myself."

"Huh?" Her reply wasn't the one he wanted to hear.

She flung an arm around his neck and sighed, again. "How do I know how I feel about anything, including you, with that madman showering me with lust? I don't trust my feelings right now. No sane person would. I need some distance from Hathaway in order to figure out where I stand." When he frowned, she reached up and traced her finger over his mouth. "Don't tell me you haven't wondered if this incredible sex and chemistry between us is normal or due to outside influence."

"Of course I've thought about it. But I'm also certain that I like being with you—even when we aren't making love."

"Yes, but you aren't the one swimming through a tidal wave of sexual distraction."

"What about right now? Are you still distracted?"

Her eyes danced with merriment. "I'm sitting on your lap naked. Why wouldn't I be distracted?"

She was pushing his limits, toying with him like a cat with cornered prey. And yet with her eyes all sparkling and her mouth edging into a grin, she was more desirable than anyone he'd ever known.

"You aren't going to give me one word of encouragement, are you?"

"How can I? It wouldn't be fair to either of us. Look," she traced a path with her finger over his neck and chest, "if I were intoxicated, you—"

"I don't take advantage of drunk women."

She shook her head. "Nor would you attempt to have a serious discussion. I'm not sure my current condition is much different. I have no idea if I'm thinking clearly. So saying anything about my feelings," she shrugged, "might be misleading at best, deceptive at worst."

"You sound logical enough to me right now, and don't forget, I'm not affected by the damn bottle."

She raised an eyebrow. "Yeah, but you're definitely affected by my actions which may all be induced by—"

"Okay. Okay. I get it." He scowled at her, more frustrated than he'd thought possible, especially when she seemed perfectly clear headed to him. "But I want you to know my feelings. You are no longer just part of the mission. In fact, I'm not certain you ever were."

"Huh?"

"I think if I'd met you under any circumstances, I'd have tried to hit on you."

"You like the way I look."

"Especially naked." He chuckled. "But I also like the way you think, even when you frustrate the hell out of me."

She gazed up at him, clearly trying not to laugh out loud, but he couldn't miss the humor in her expression. "Now that's a backhanded compliment I've never heard before."

"I'm trying to have a serious conversation."

"Really."

"And it's difficult enough without your sass."

"Is that so?"

"I like you, Amanda." He combed his fingers through his hair and stared at her. "I like you a lot."

"Ditto." She didn't even hesitate, and his hopes for them rose. He knew her well enough by now to realize she didn't say things lightly.

He kept his tone casual and upbeat. "We're going to spend time together when this mission is over."

She grinned. "That sounded like a demand."

"Oh, it was. I can be very demanding." He lifted her off his lap and set her onto her feet. "And right now we should continue searching this apartment. The sooner we find the bottle—"

"And figure out who murdered my sister."

"—the sooner the mission will be over and we can move on with our lives."

"Can't we enjoy the moment?" Her tone was easy,

but he glimpsed shadowed pain in her eyes before she turned away, giving him a hint that she may have kept the conversation on the surface, but her feelings ran deeper. And experience told him she had reservations, but whether they were about him, her, or their situation he couldn't discern.

While she washed, collected her clothes and dressed, he did the same. Both of them continued their search, but he looked for hiding places automatically, his mind on Amanda.

Women were the more complicated of the sexes. He'd always known that. But comparing his sisters to Amanda was like equating a step into a rain puddle with plunging into a riptide. And he was having difficulty keeping his head above water, never mind swimming ashore to safety.

He wouldn't have minded diving in—if he could be certain they were doing so together. But while the lovely Amanda was giving him his every sexual fantasy, he longed for the intimacy of knowing she was being washed away right alongside him.

Perhaps he should try harder to convince her that they belonged together, but he had too much pride for that. He wanted her to be with him due to her own desires, not his urging.

He'd had a few flings in his life but none of the other women had excited or intrigued him as Amanda had. They were good together and it irked him that she wouldn't admit it. Almost as if she feared...

God, no. Please don't let her be one of those women who couldn't commit.

Surely, she was stronger than that?

Bolt recalled the pain in her eyes and wondered who or what had caused it. He liked knowing his opponent. He couldn't fight a memory or an uncertainty—not unless he knew and understood exactly what it was.

But she wouldn't talk to him about her feelings. Stubborn, proud, independent, Amanda certainly had gotten under his skin. And "like" wasn't a strong enough word. He cared about her. He was beginning to think about living together. About taking her to meet the family. About how she'd fit in with his friends.

His friends would adore her. Every one of them liked strong women. His sisters and mom were another matter. He never could predict their reactions. But while he preferred that they adore Amanda as he did, he wouldn't necessarily change his mind if they didn't. Sure, approval would be great, but Bolt had a mind of his own. And he knew he wanted Amanda in his life. She felt right. End of story.

Now all he had to do was get her to agree. Right now, the task seemed impossible. She wasn't going to budge until they finished the mission. And while he was eager to move on with his life, contradictorily, he didn't want his search for the bottle to end. The more time he spent with Amanda, the more time he had to convince her that they were good for one another, meant for one another.

They still had several hours to search Hathaway's private quarters. While the times when Hathaway's staff were gone was rare, he didn't rush. If necessary, the Shey Group could create other opportunities.

Amanda searched the bathroom while Bolt checked the giant closet. The space was larger than most living rooms. Hathaway had an entire rack filled with dozens of shoes—loafers, dress shoes and sneakers—in an assortment of colors and styles. All his shirts hung on one long wall, the colors sorted from light to dark, and he must have had a dozen shirts in various hues of purple alone. Another wall held suits, jackets and slacks, all made of the finest materials. Hathaway even had a rack for belts and ties.

Bolt pressed the button, and as the ties fluttered by, he glimpsed an anomaly in the wall paneling. He stopped the tie rack from rotating and carefully felt the wooden panels for a latch. Nothing. The wall felt as smooth as Amanda's skin, though nowhere as soft.

There.

His fingers snagged on a crease in the wood. "Amanda. I've found something."

"I'll be right there." Her voice rose in excitement. "Did you find the bottle?"

11

AMAZED THAT ANYONE required such an extensive wardrobe, Amanda hurried through the oversize walk-in closet past the suits, shirt, jackets and shoes. After the amazing late-afternoon delights she'd shared with Bolt, her steps were still a bit unsteady, her conflicting emotions a riot of wonder and wariness—and joy that Bolt wanted to continue their relationship. Perhaps because she was unaccustomed to following her own preferences without having to consider how they would affect Donna, or maybe because the splendid lovemaking had come before deeper feelings had surfaced, she'd never felt so free to explore what she wanted from a man.

Amanda could please herself. It was as if she were on a vacation, where whatever she did with Bolt wouldn't affect her real life. She was excited about the prospect of extending their relationship and time together. And yet, her practical nature warned her that Bolt was too good to be true. And she feared that when the bottle stopped altering her and the danger ended, she might not find Bolt as terrific as she did right now.

Clearly he'd wanted answers from her. She didn't

want to encourage him and then go back on her word if she felt differently once she was away from Hathaway's influence. Yet, she suspected that finishing the mission might come sooner than she'd expected, especially after hearing the elation in Bolt's tone.

She rounded a corner in the L-shaped closet and his broad shoulders blocked most of her view. But from her vantage point she could see that he'd found and opened a secret compartment. And when he stepped back, she got her first look at the perfume bottle. Blue, delicate and trimmed with a silver filigree it appeared old, but ordinary. She'd expected an aura or supernatural light to surround it, but there was nothing obvious to indicate the bottle had extraordinary powers.

When Bolt didn't reach for it, she frowned. "Is that the right bottle?"

"Yes."

"So, now what? Do you call the police?" Amanda realized that his mission was over. Yet, once he reported that he'd found the stolen bottle in Hathaway's quarters, Hathaway would blame her for suggesting he hire "Bob Timmins" and for bringing him here. He'd certainly fire her, ruining her cover and her investigation. And likely he'd claim he hadn't known the bottle was stolen. She doubted he'd even be arrested for theft. Which meant he'd get off scot-free for both crimes.

Bolt shook his head. "Our client wants the bottle returned to the rightful owner. Calling the law isn't my job. But if I retrieve the bottle now, Hathaway's going to know that we aren't who we seem to be."

"But your mission will be accomplished."

"Yours won't be." To her astonishment, Bolt carefully closed and latched the sliding panel. "We'll come back for the bottle after you nail him for Donna's murder."

"You'd delay your mission for me?" Stunned, Amanda shoved her hair out of her eyes to find Bolt smiling down at her. She hadn't expected such a magnanimous gesture. The FBI didn't work this way. With the Bureau, the mission objective always came first. "What if your boss finds out?"

"Kincaid won't mind."

"You're going to tell him?" Her lower jaw dropped.

Bolt laughed. "It's a perfume bottle, not a life and death decision. It's not as though Hathaway's planning to give it away or sell it."

"But we don't know that. And you've gone to so much trouble. Recruiting me. My cover. The expense of the suite and the surveillance equipment. Are you certain your boss won't fire you?"

Bolt snapped open his phone and dialed. They waited as the encryption program rerouted through various countries and satellites took a minute or two, time she needed to collect her wits. Bolt seemed so confident his boss would go along with his change of plan, yet she knew he was taking a huge risk to help her. He was making the offer as if it was nothing. And unbelievably, he wasn't asking her for anything in return.

"This is Bolt. I'm turning on the speaker phone so Amanda can listen. We've located the perfume bottle."

"Good." Logan Kincaid's voice rang through as crisp and clear as though he was in the next room.

"I'm leaving the bottle in a hidden cubbyhole of Hathaway's closet while we investigate Donna's murder."

"Understood."

That's it? Amanda would have had to answer a dozen questions from her boss, who would have then passed the request up the ladder. She'd have had a decision in days. Clearly the FBI and the Shey Group operated very differently. And she couldn't have been more appreciative.

"Thank you, sir." Amanda spoke into the speaker of the cell phone, but kept her message brief due to the lump in her throat. She felt as though she was an emotional bouncing ball—one moment sky high, the next plummeting. She'd certainly lucked out when it came to Bolt and the Shey Group, and her hope of solving Donna's murder soared. As the two men cleared up a few details, she marveled over Bolt's behavior. No one had ever done anything like this for her before.

She understood why Bolt gave Logan Kincaid his loyalty. And she was glad people like these men worked to keep their country safe. But even better, she was proud that Bolt had been chosen by such an exclusive organization. And that such a good man like Bolt wanted her made Amanda sigh. She had to be a fool to keep putting Bolt off in the emotional department. Okay, a complete idiot.

If Donna had been alive, she would have told Amanda that she was insane to hold back where Bolt was concerned. Yet, Amanda was of the mindset that first appearances could be deceiving. It was her nature to be cautious. Yet, she and Bolt were way beyond first appearances and the harder she looked at the man, the better he seemed.

He was gorgeous, hot, hunky. But he was also kind, playful and protective. And he liked her intelligence. She'd never had a true partner to work with before and she had to admit she was enjoying the experience on several levels. She respected his skills as an operative, but she liked the companionship, too.

For the first time, working with a partner seemed like a better idea than working alone. She could bounce ideas off of Bolt without wondering if he'd think less of her. He never put her down. And he always remained upbeat and on her side.

Her heart lighter than it had been in months, she supposed she'd better start making up for lost time. The moment he hung up with Kincaid, she flung her arms around his neck and kissed him. "Thanks."

Bolt grinned. "You're welcome."

"I would never have asked you to put back the bottle."

"I know." He wrapped his arms around her. "That's why it was so much fun to surprise you."

"I'm glad you did." She wriggled against him. "What other surprises have you got for me?"

FINDING FRANCES TURNED out to be easy. The arrogant model was in Boston for a photo shoot. But when even getting her on the phone to ask her about the diary Melanie had told them about proved to be impossible,

Amanda and Bolt turned their attention to searching for Melanie Carter. Since Bolt's computer program hadn't yet given them any leads, they began with the return address on the envelope of the letter Melanie had written to Hathaway.

Although they'd learned more about Melanie's background since their initial conversation, after finding her letter to Hathaway, Amanda had a lot more questions. Had Melanie been jealous of Donna's relationship with Hathaway? Jealous enough to kill? Or did Melanie also suspect Hathaway, was afraid of him, and wanted to make him pay for what he'd done to Donna?

They discovered that right after Melanie's accident and her return from the two months she'd spent in the hospital recuperating, Melanie had moved on but left a forwarding address. A Shey agent had traced the ex-model to a seedy apartment in the Bronx, which they immediately set off for. When they knocked on the door, she opened it and didn't seem especially surprised to see them. But Amanda wasn't taking anything for granted. As a model, the woman could control her expressions.

"Did you find Hathaway's diary?" Melanie asked as she gestured for them to enter.

Amanda shook her head and stepped inside with Bolt just behind her. The apartment was small, but surprisingly comfortable and homey, with potted plants, a homemade afghan thrown over a leather sofa and the scent of hot soup coming from the kitchen. Cheerful curtains hung over the windows, their honey color set off by the burnished, aged wooden walls and the glow of several art deco style lamps. The old building even boasted a fireplace. Melanie had a framed picture of herself and Hathaway above the mantel.

Seeing her glance, Melanie sighed and rubbed her neck. "Those were happier times."

"We found a letter you wrote to Hathaway asking him for money." Amanda took the lead in the conversation as she and Bolt had previously agreed. They didn't want the woman to feel as though the two of them were ganging up on her.

Melanie perched on the edge of her chair as if she was going to stand and flee at any moment. "After I was injured, Hathaway conveniently forgot he owed me money from a month's work I'd done for the agency."

"So you were trying to collect what he owed you?" While Amanda didn't fully trust the woman, she sounded sincere and her story fit the known facts, so Amanda was inclined to believe her. She now suspected Melanie hadn't been strong-arming Hathaway, and her sympathy for the woman escalated. For Hathaway to treat an injured ex-employee so badly infuriated her, for him to do so to his ex-lover was incredibly cold and cruel.

Melanie nodded, twisting her fingers together in her lap and avoiding Amanda's gaze. Amanda proceeded as gently as possible. "Did you ever collect?"

Melanie hesitated, the look in her eyes turning dreamy. "Hathaway told me he'd pay me what he owed and a large bonus if I did one more job for him."

"You agreed?" Amanda guessed.

"That was when I foolishly had hopes that Hathaway could overlook my injury and we could get back together."

"You loved him. Any woman might have done the same," Amanda said softly, sympathetically.

"At one of his parties, Hathaway heard about a priceless perfume bottle that he absolutely had to own. After I…offered to acquire it for him, he was very pleased to take my phone calls again." In contrast to her words, Melanie's face saddened and a tear escaped her eye. Angrily she wiped it away. "I can't believe I was so stupid. He didn't want me. He was using me and my contacts."

"Your contacts?"

"I grew up poor. In the Bronx. But then I made a name for myself with my modeling. I was a success, in love, on top of the world. I thought the money would never end and I never kept track of it as I should have." She raised her head and stared out the window. "Who would have thought I'd end up back here in the old neighborhood?"

"But what did you mean by contacts?"

"This neighborhood has criminal elements. It wasn't too difficult to hook up with a few guys." She sniffed. "I knew better. I never should have helped him."

"So you stole the bottle and then Hathaway paid you?"

"Yes. I'd never done anything criminal before—but I was desperate to get the bill collectors off my back. And I hoped I could prove that I was still useful to Hathaway."

"Do you know why he wanted the perfume bottle so badly?" Amanda asked.

"He never said. I thought maybe he wanted to manufacture the perfume—especially after he hired Donna. But I don't know. Everything got so crazy. I'd always loved Hathaway, but after he possessed the perfume bottle, he began to act strangely."

"What do you mean?"

"Like he was a sheikh and every woman was part of his harem. Like he was a king and every female was his handmaiden. And women responded just like I did. They gave him whatever he asked for. Their bodies. Their hearts."

"That must have been painful for you."

"Despite the other women, I became desperate to see him. I can't explain my behavior. It was an irresistible compulsion. I spied on him. Even after learning that half the women in New York had suddenly gone as ga-ga as I had over the man, I still wanted him, but I also hated him. I wasn't myself."

"I'm so sorry." Amanda was no longer pretending. Hathaway had treated Melanie terribly and she wondered if he'd done the same to her sister.

"And I was so jealous that I made myself ill. Especially after he took up with Frances. That bitch took over my modeling jobs and my man, but then Hathaway dropped her, too." Melanie's voice shook. "Frances was furious when Hathaway moved on to your sister. That's when she came to me with a plan for revenge."

"Against Donna?"

"No. Against Hathaway. She claimed he had a diary where he wrote down all his dark secrets. If we could steal it, we could force Hathaway to do what we wanted."

"Which was what exactly?" Bolt asked, interrupting for the first time.

Melanie didn't seem to mind. And Amanda appreciated his help.

Melanie shrugged, then winced and rubbed her neck again. "We didn't really have a plan. At least I didn't. I think Frances planned to see what was actually in the diary before we took the next step. Meanwhile, I let Frances talk me into befriending Donna in the hopes of finding out where Hathaway kept his diary. But in reality, I liked hearing what Hathaway was doing and with whom—even if it was painful. It was like I had a sickness in my blood for that man."

"Did my sister find the diary?"

"I'm not certain. She told me over the phone that she had had a fight with Hathaway over the perfume bottle when he wanted her to analyze the chemical formula instead of model. I was supposed to meet her the next day. And then she was dead."

Amanda thanked the woman for her honesty and they left the apartment. After hearing the story, Amanda was inclined to believe every word. She suspected Melanie had told them the truth, just not all of it. Bolt took her hand and she appreciated the gesture. The talk about her sister's death upset her—especially since they seemed no closer to finding a way to prove Hathaway had committed murder than when they'd begun.

They strode down the tree-shaded sidewalk to the corner where they would catch a cab back to Manhattan. Bolt steered her around several wide cracks in the cement where grass had grown through and past a couple walking their golden retriever.

"Hathaway and the bottle made her act like that—I almost told her. Poor woman, she can't figure out why she still wanted the man, even after he'd been so cruel."

"You could have told her."

"She probably wouldn't have believed me. And then she might have thought we were nuts and stopped talking."

He squeezed her hand. "You did great with her."

"Thanks. You don't suppose Hathaway would have been stupid enough to murder my sister and then confess in a diary, do you?"

"Under normal circumstances, I wouldn't think so. But many egomaniacs do stupid things. Look at the Nixon tapes. If he'd wiped them clean, he wouldn't have had to resign the Presidency. Often people in powerful positions believe they are indestructible."

"I hope you're right. Again."

"Again?" They'd almost reached the corner, but Bolt halted, seeming in no hurry to catch a cab. In the crisp fall air, the turning leaves were a perfect background for his burnished skin. Dappled light slipping through the tree branches lit the confusion in his gaze.

"You're right about us."

He quirked an eyebrow. "Care to elaborate?"

"We've been away from Hathaway for a while now and his bottle, and my feelings haven't changed."

"Oh, so you do have feelings for me?" he teased. "I was beginning to wonder if you'd ever admit them to yourself, much less me."

"Well, I still can't be one hundred percent certain. The bottle could have lingering effects. However, I will admit I like having you around."

Happiness welled up inside her. She was glad he'd had the confidence to believe in them despite the circumstances.

His hand clamped down on her shoulder and gently turned her. "What else do you feel about me?"

She squirmed a little inside. She didn't like talking about her emotions. Saying aloud what she felt made everything real, gave everything consequence. She much preferred to keep everything up in the air. But she knew she couldn't keep a man like Bolt dangling forever and she didn't want to risk losing him because she couldn't change. Her focus had always been on Donna, then work, work, work. Sure, she was scared of allowing herself to love. After all, she'd lost her parents. Then Donna. Loving was scary.

"Come on, give it up to me." His tone remained light but his gaze was serious.

"When our parents died, I wanted to shut down and grieve, but I couldn't. I poured all my energy into building a future for Donna and me. After she died, I threw myself into work while I healed. And now that she's been gone for a while, I've realized how much I changed after our parents died. I became the responsible and practical one."

"You had no choice."

"But I closed myself off—though I allowed myself to love Donna of course."

"And she left you, too." Bolt opened his arms wide and gave her a comforting bear hug. "I'm not going anywhere. But I'm sure you know there are no guarantees—especially in my line of work."

"I've healed enough to accept that." She nestled into his strength, wondering how he always knew exactly what she needed. "I used to think that if I lost one more person who was close to me, I'd break. But I wouldn't. I'd grieve, but I could go on."

"Life has made you strong. Another person would have fallen apart after her parents died, but you grew up fast and took over. And when Donna died, you didn't go into a depression, you started investigating. Your way of coping is to 'do' something. That's rare, and it shows courage."

She choked on words that had to be said. "So I'm open to letting myself care about you. I just hope…"

"Are you worried that you can't think clearly due to Hathaway and the perfume bottle?"

"That, too."

"What else?"

"I'm afraid to let my feelings escalate."

"Because of my profession?"

She shook her head. Although working for the Shey Group put his life in danger, she believed that superior abilities like his would keep him safe. "I'm bad luck."

"What?"

He gripped her shoulders and separated them so he could see her face. She didn't want to meet his gaze but forced herself to do so and she saw no disgust, just puzzlement.

"I didn't know practical Amanda was superstitious."

"Neither did I. But deep down I'm quite certain that if you and I…if we remain together…something will happen to you and it will be my fault." She shook her hair from her eyes. "It's not rational. But it's how I feel. And no matter how many times I tell myself I'm being ridiculous, it doesn't change anything."

He didn't make fun of her, but appeared to be thinking hard. "I'm not a shrink but do you blame yourself for your parents' and Donna's deaths?"

"Not my parents'. But Donna was my responsibility. I should have talked her out of working for Hathaway."

"She was a grown woman. It was her choice."

"I know." She rubbed her temple and grinned. "I'm a mess. I don't know why you put up with me."

"Me, either."

She slipped her hands around his back and raised her lips for a kiss. "But I'm glad you do."

HATHAWAY WAS DISTRACTED. Amanda was a puzzle that he couldn't solve, and he didn't like mysteries. Why was she beyond his control? How was she resisting him?

At first he feared the power of the perfume bottle had a finite usage. But his powers still worked with every other woman. In fact, Frances had phoned him twice from Boston, claiming she just had to see him.

So what was different about Amanda? Even the brilliant Donna had succumbed to his charms.

Building his empire had been difficult. Yet, he'd succeeded and intended to stay on top. He liked that *Peo-*

ple magazine had included a four-page layout about his agency, enjoyed being seen and photographed with the world's most beautiful women. And he most especially relished the way all of them clamored to join him in bed.

And no one was going to take from him what he'd worked so hard to build. Not Donna, who'd betrayed him. Certainly not Amanda who was so good at resisting him. Her ability enraged him. He'd had difficulty putting on a front for the Broadway opening he was attending. At least once they'd entered the theater, he'd been able to drop the pleasant expression he'd had to put on for the press. The paparazzi had been anxious to snap his picture with his newest ingenue.

Once they'd been seated in his private box, she'd gone down on her knees for him, but he couldn't get hard. And although he blamed her lack of skill, he knew better. The reason for his sudden impotence was Amanda's fault. It was her he wanted on her knees. And by God, he would have her.

But how?

He had no doubts he had affected her. But she always escaped before she gave in to her own desires. He needed a scheme to keep her in his presence long enough for the bottle to do its work.

He grunted, pulled the ingenue from the floor and calmly rezipped his pants. Amanda would soon be taking care of him. He'd phone her and order her to his private suite. He'd give his employees the day off, not that they would talk. He paid them too well—in money and sex.

However, the lovely Amanda might run or scream.

He would prevent both. But rape wasn't his thing. He liked the power of compelling women to come to him—especially against their will.

The notion of Amanda being unable to resist him did what the ingenue could not. He thought of Amanda ripping off her clothes, dancing naked to entice him, then imagined refusing to ease her needs, and he grew aroused.

He shot a measure of lust at the woman beside him, then tugged the confused model back to the floor. When she took him into her mouth, he fantasized that Amanda was giving him a blow job.

Soon his desire would come true. And since the first time a woman gave in to him was always the best, he intended to preserve the memory. He'd buy the new digital video camera he'd been ogling. He shouldn't deny himself. He would have Amanda and then he'd enjoy watching her yield to him in close up.

Barely refraining from rubbing his hands together with glee, Hathaway carefully made his plans. He'd have to send Bob Timmins to another location. Although Hathaway had ordered Amanda to watch the man, he didn't like the way Timmins was always close to her. He struck Hathaway as the kind of man who would risk his life to protect a woman and he had far too much physical prowess to take lightly.

Hathaway was also suspicious that she was a bit too aware of him. He was younger than Hathaway. Although his other women preferred Hathaway to husbands and lovers, Amanda might be infatuated with Timmins. She certainly hadn't seemed to mind when he'd told her she'd be spending so much time with the man.

Best to send Timmins away. And then Hathaway would make his move.

Tomorrow was going to be the day. A day Amanda would never forget.

12

AMANDA WOKE UP to the cell phone ringing in her ear. Fumbling for the phone in the darkness, she squinted at the time on the display—5:00 a.m. She groggily answered, "Hello," then wished she hadn't.

Beside her, Bolt didn't move but she knew he was awake from the tension in his muscles. Odd, how she'd gotten to know him so well in such a short period of time that she recognized his body's signals.

"I need you here, ASAP." Hathaway's voice sounded harried and cranky.

Now what? "What's wrong?" she asked, trying to put concern into her tone, when all she wanted to do was cuddle up with Bolt and return to her dreams.

"Everything's wrong. Be here soon. Call Bob Timmins and get him here, too." Hathaway hung up with a click and the dial tone droned rudely in her ear.

With a groan, Amanda rolled over, her hair fanning over Bolt's chest, her head pillowed by his comfortable shoulder. "I need more sleep. Another five hours would do the trick."

"But you don't have five hours?" Bolt guessed, sounding wide awake and perky.

She wouldn't be awake until she drank a triple espresso. In the meantime, she snuggled against Bolt's warmth. And he tugged the cover off.

"Hey," she complained, reaching to pull it back, but her fingers couldn't quite reach it without getting out of bed.

He laughed. How anyone could awaken in such a good mood was beyond her comprehension, especially when he'd gotten as little sleep as she had. "Your boss awaits."

"I'm too sleepy. It's dark. I can't see," she mumbled, suspecting she wasn't quite coherent. Bolt had seen her at her worst already. Without makeup. Without brushing her teeth or combing her hair. And now he also knew that she wasn't a morning person. But her bad side never seemed to deter him.

He shook her shoulder. "Why don't you try opening your eyes, darling?"

However, she could do without such persistence. "Mmm."

He rolled from bed and her head slid onto the pillow. She immediately missed his warmth and burrowed into the spot where his body heat still remained. When he turned on a light and a radio, she screwed her eyes tightly shut and pulled the pillow over her head to block out sound and light.

When he left, she heard him pad into the bathroom and turn on the shower, and she almost fell back asleep. But then his strong arms were lifting her, carrying her, setting her down. She refused to open her eyes. But when warm water cascaded over her, she glared at him and sputtered. "What the hell are you doing?"

"And good morning to you, too."

"How can you sound so happy…"

He pulled her against his chest, supported her while hot water rained down her back, and he rubbed soap over her shoulders. She could think of worse ways to wake up.

"I'm not at my best first thing in the morning."

"No kidding."

He was laughing at her and she didn't care. If she couldn't go back to sleep, then showering with him would be next on her list. Even as he worked the soap into a lather and the spicy aroma enticed her nostrils, his slippery fingers found every knotted muscle and cleverly kneaded them into submission.

"Oh, you feel so good."

"I could feel better."

She wriggled her hips against him. "Do we have time?"

"We'll make time. Hathaway isn't going to fire you today for coming in a few minutes later than he expects."

"Why not?"

She leaned back and appreciated Bolt's hands as he slid the soapy warmth of his palms over her breasts. Already her sleepiness was receding and giving way to the urge to make love. Bolt was ever inventive. She liked when he made love to her slowly and she liked the opposite, too, when he was quick and hard. She liked him, period.

"I saw Hathaway's schedule. There's a fashion show downtown and his models are headlining."

"He's probably got a dozen errands for me to run and

more security checks for you." She'd worked for Hathaway long enough to know he thought everything was an emergency, everything had to be done now—but the truth of the matter was he simply liked to keep his employees at his beck and call.

But none of that seemed to matter right now now with the rising fever simmering in her blood. Bolt had so quickly learned what she liked, how she liked to be touched and where. Even as he turned her to wash away the soap from her breasts, he was moving to her bottom, between her thighs, her legs and toes.

When he finished soaping and rinsing her, she was aroused enough to demand he give her the soap. And then it was her turn to skim her hands over his delicious body. To taunt and tease and trust him to allow her to do as she wished with his powerful shoulders, broad chest and six-pack abs. He really had a great body with muscles in all the right places.

When she heard her cell phone ring with demanding persistence, she ignored Hathaway, the only person rude enough to call at such an ungodly hour. He probably needed coffee made or wanted to make sure the carpet was clean. This was their time—hers and Bolt's—and she intended to make the most of it.

Today would be long and trying. She owed herself a chance to fortify her reserves. And nobody was better at giving her what she needed than Bolt.

Although she adored making love to him, their relationship had moved beyond lust. It now encompassed her feelings for him and his for her in ways she hadn't anticipated. Who would have thought she would worry what Bolt thought about when Hathaway turned her on? This early in the morning, her situation was too odd for her to contemplate with much clarity. But her circumstances were abnormal and she felt as though she had been picked up by a tornado and was spinning out of control.

She only knew if the situation were reversed, if some other woman could use odd powers to excite Bolt, Amanda would be very unhappy. She'd doubt his feelings for her. Luckily Bolt was strong enough for both of them. Not once had he ever indicated that she was weak or that her feelings for him were less because she had difficulty dealing with Hathaway.

That Bolt made damn sure she wasn't left alone with the man was part of his job on this mission—but it also suited his own interests as well as hers. She simply had to trust that he could keep protecting her from Hathaway, a man who the more she got to know, the more she despised.

But her thoughts about Hathaway washed down the drain as Bolt took over her senses. With his hands on her body, his lips on hers and her body begging for sweet release, she lost all awareness of time. She had no idea when he'd donned the condom. She could think only of Bolt's hands on her hips as he lifted her. And she parted her thighs as he ever-so-slowly lowered her onto his erection. Once he'd filled her, she wrapped her legs around his waist, her arms around his neck and raised her mouth for a kiss.

She wanted every inch of her skin to be touching his. And as his tongue fused with hers, as her senses spun deliciously out of control, she clung to him, wishing they could stay in this suite and make love all day and night. He cupped her bottom and she braced her feet against the shower wall. And they moved as one, riding together through the storm, the whirlwind of wanting spiraling through her until her heart thundered and her blood ran wild.

And when she found delicious, intoxicating release, she threw back her head and opened her eyes to lock gazes with Bolt. He tensed and poured into her, but the intimacy of his look at the moment of climax shocked her.

Because in addition to his passion, his eyes were filled with unmistakable love.

THROUGHOUT THE LONG DAY, Amanda fortified herself with the memory of Bolt's searing look. It carried her through Hathaway's innuendos and demands and dozens of minor emergencies that had started at 6:00 a.m. with his stolen limo. It sailed her past the enormous difficulty of coordinating dozens of last-minute details with the hotel, the designers and the models. The work was exhausting and time-consuming and left her no time for private moments with Bolt, who was busy with security.

But her priorities were changing. Work was no longer preventing her feelings from emerging. Not only was Bolt constantly slipping into her thoughts as she worked, she was missing him.

The event would take place in the same hotel where they'd met, at the street level of Hathaway's offices. And after finding the bottle and suspecting Hathaway needed a certain proximity to it to use his powers, she knew why he rarely left the building that included his office, personal suite and hotel.

The mega skyscrapers were almost a self-contained city with shops and restaurants inside. But despite her many trips up and down and through vast lobbies, she still struggled with a cloying claustrophobia. It wasn't as if the walls were closing in, but that Hathaway was. He had a certain vibe, and a certain look in his eye that warned her he was up to something. Yet, surrounded by dozens of people, she should have felt safe.

But her gut churned and, as she hunted down a missing shipment of shoes that hadn't shown up with the dresses, she wondered if she would ever find out what had happened to her sister. All her efforts didn't seem to be leading her in the direction she needed and she had to keep reminding herself that each task kept her in Hathaway's employ, which was the only way to keep her moving toward her goal.

Her phone seemed to ring every five minutes with another problem that Hathaway needed her to solve. A model needed aspirin from the pharmacy, a special powder. The flowers in the ballroom were droopy and needed watering. Would she call the florist? The printed sheets for the buyers were the wrong color. And the air-conditioning hadn't been turned down. There weren't enough chairs and the aisles were too wide. The place would look empty. A reporter needed a photopass left at the registration desk and someone had dirtied the carpet and the hotel needed to clean it immediately.

During the day, she wondered if anyone without ulterior motives would work for Hathaway. He didn't pay well enough to inspire this kind of madcap working pace. Demanding, autocratic, he seemed to believe that the harder he drove his people the more successful he would be.

But everyone was stressed. After a designer screamed at a model for gaining weight and ruining the lines of his dress, the model broke into tears. Every time the makeup artist fixed her face she began crying again. Backstage was chaos. Clothing racks wheeled back and forth by assistants never seemed to be in the right place.

Then the sound system came on so loud it almost blew out Amanda's eardrums. And the lighting check left her with spots in her vision and a blazing headache. She stopped at a water fountain to down two aspirin and leaned against the wall to take a well-earned breather.

Of course, that was the moment Hathaway chose to find her. He swaggered down the hall like a king who expected his subjects to scurry out of the way. Most did. Amanda remained against the wall, praying he wouldn't notice her.

But he stopped and she figured he was about to call her out for taking a break. But he lowered his voice so only she could hear. "Where's Bob Timmins?"

Bolt? "I'm not certain. Why?"

"The police have found my limo. There's been damage to the computer system and I want him to check that

Uncontrollable

out as well as sweep the vehicle for bugs." He plucked a paper from his right breast pocket and pressed it into her hand. "The vehicle is being repaired at that address. Find Timmins and have him see to it immediately."

She thought of the myriad of tasks she still had to finish before the fashion show began and realized that she couldn't go with Bolt. She checked the address and saw that the limo wasn't even in Manhattan, but Staten Island. Bolt would be gone for hours.

"If you want me to stick with him, you'll need someone else to take over here for me."

"We'll have to trust him to go alone and do his job. You did say he was capable." Hathaway didn't wait for her answer, but moved down the hall, a man certain his orders would be followed to the letter.

Confused by the sudden change in plans, she dialed Bolt's cell phone. Hathaway had originally told her to watch Bolt because he didn't trust him. So what had changed? She didn't get it. "Bolt?"

"I heard." She fingered the pin at her collar.

Amanda gave Bolt the address. "If you don't go, it will blow your cover."

"I don't want to leave you alone." At Bolt's admission, her heart warmed. She liked having him worry over her because he cared—not because he feared she couldn't handle herself.

"I should be fine for the duration of the show. Hathaway will be in the limelight and surrounded by his adoring public. He seems to pull his stunts only within the privacy of his home or office."

"He might still find a few minutes to get you alone."

"I don't think so. He wouldn't risk it. There's too much to do. Too many people around."

"You're probably right."

"But?" She heard the reluctance in Bolt's voice.

"I don't like it."

"Neither do I," she admitted, her pulse elevating. "Over how long a distance will this transmitter work?"

"It might reach most of Manhattan. Not all the way to Staten Island."

So not only would Bolt be far away, he'd be out of touch. A spike of cold shimmied along her spine, but she fought down her apprehension. She patted her thigh and her gun reassured her. "Get back as soon as you can, okay?"

"No problem."

With a sigh of resignation, she shut off her phone, pushed away from the hall and almost bumped into the arrogant Frances Ledan. The model's eyes sharpened when she spied Amanda. "Just the person I was looking for."

Amanda hadn't seen the model since she'd left for Boston. She'd wanted to ask her more about Hathaway's private habits, especially his diary, but the busy hallway leading to the side entrance to tonight's show was not the right place. As if by mutual consent the two women walked out of the building and onto the sidewalk. Amanda had to step smartly to keep up with the long-legged beauty, but with her curiosity leaping, she was re-energized.

"How was Boston?"

"Snobby. Boring."

"Sorry." Traffic sped by and the crowded sidewalk of disinterested strangers gave them the illusion of privacy. Amanda hadn't forgotten that Frances had openly admitted that Hathaway had told her what to say the last time they'd spoken. The woman was an enigma, playing her own game. "So what's up?"

"Hathaway wants you to join him in his quarters for a party tonight."

Amanda frowned. "I just saw him. He didn't mention it to me."

"He wants you to wear something special tonight for the fashion show. And he requested that you not change before his celebration party."

If Amanda had been wearing her normal clothes, she would have understood Hathaway's request. But the Shey Group had supplied her with a wardrobe in the height of fashion. Hathaway had no reason to be ashamed of her clothing.

Suspicion made her ask, "Will you be at the party?"

Frances raised one haughty eyebrow. "Of course. The entire office staff and all the models are invited. We all wait for the midnight papers and the social papers to come out—just like for a Broadway show."

"All right then."

Frances suddenly pulled her close. "Be careful. He wants you badly."

"Tell me something I don't already know."

"He's willing to go further than you'd think to have you," Frances warned.

"Why are you telling me this?" she asked, sensing no friendliness in the other woman.

"I'd be fired if I didn't."

"I don't understand." But Amanda did. Hathaway was warning her with all the audacity of a man certain that she'd be unable to resist. He was testing her.

"I have to go." Frances turned on a four-inch spiked heel, dismissing her.

"Wait. One second," Amanda demanded, suddenly remembering why she'd wanted to talk to Frances in the first place. "Does Hathaway keep a diary?"

But her question came too late. Frances had already hurried away.

BOLT RENTED A CAR to drive to Staten Island, found the garage easily and parked across the street. He'd had the Shey Group check the police report and learned that Hathaway had pulled strings to keep the vehicle from being impounded. As he neared, he saw no damage, no dents, no broken windows, not even a scratch on the glossy white paint. But a mechanic was under the raised hood, checking the oil, which he found odd. Why would the guy be doing routine maintenance?

Out of habit, Bolt took in his surroundings. Two other mechanics stood outside the garage, smoking cigarettes. It appeared normal, yet his suspicions had gone to full alert. He'd expected damage to the limo and the routine of the oil change alerted him that all was not as it seemed.

When the two mechanics on cigarette break approached, Bolt kept them in sight, noting that they moved with a lithe grace that suggested martial arts training. By the size of their biceps bulging under their uniforms, these guys had some muscle on them, too. As they approached he noted their hands. He saw no grease under the nails and calluses along the ridges and his wariness ratcheted up another notch.

This was a setup. Hathaway had sent him out here on a wild goose chase to prevent him from protecting Amanda. The realization raced through his mind at the same moment the guy checking the oil drew a gun and aimed it at Bolt.

Big mistake.

Bolt slammed the hood down on the man's arm. Bone crunched. With a scream, he dropped the gun and the bullet he fired whizzed harmlessly by Bolt's ear. One down, two to go. The pair of mechanics approached warily but with the confidence of men certain of their abilities.

One bent and slid a knife from his boot. The other advanced to attack with a jab to the jaw. Bolt's catlike reflexes and hand-to-hand combat experience stood him in good stead. He hadn't fought for his life in years but the instincts and muscle memory kicked in. He shifted, side-kicked the man's knee, a dirty fighting move that was efficient, but not deadly. His opponent went down with a satisfying thud.

Bolt wished he had time to draw his gun. But the third opponent with the knife lunged in, slicing from side to side and displaying a keen knowledge of knife fighting.

If the man gave him one extra second, Bolt would

have gone for his gun. But he required his hands for defense, and if he tried for his weapon, dropping his guard for that brief moment would likely be the last thing he ever did. The knife fighter would seek the opening and split him open from neck to gut.

Even a defensive wound on the wrist could be deadly, due to massive amounts of blood loss. As Bolt backed away, giving himself more room to fight, he considered running straight for his car. But if his opponent could throw the knife as well as he could fight, that option wouldn't succeed, either.

Better to circle, wait for an opening. He watched the knife fighter's eyes, not his hands, waiting for the moment of attack. The two men circled, sizing up one another with the experience of battle-hardened pros.

One slip, one stumble and the other man would be all over him like a wild dog on raw steak. And he wouldn't just lose the fight and possibly his life, he would be letting Amanda down. There was no guessing what that bastard Hathaway intended to do with her.

His opponent feinted to the right. But Bolt didn't take the bait.

Patience.

Watch the eyes.

Wait for the real attack.

He didn't consider any move but a defensive one, balanced with a counterstrike. The main rule of knife fighting was to first disarm, then disable. And the men were too well matched in ability for Bolt to become an aggressor when he didn't also have a knife in hand.

Focus.

Wait for an opening.

Wait for the eyes to give him a clue.

Seconds ticked by and his awareness that every movement delayed his return to Amanda had his nerves on edge. He couldn't force the fight or he'd end up dead and a dead protector was useless to help her.

For the first time, Bolt's opponent glanced down at his hand—the warning sign he'd been watching for. His opponent wanted to sneak in the knife without suffering a counterattack from Bolt's fist. And that concern gave away his intention to commit to a full attack.

Bolt tensed on the balls of his feet. Hands open, wrists cocked, he didn't so much as blink. And his opponent didn't disappoint him. He lunged. And sliced.

Bolt moved inside the attack, captured the wrist, viciously twisted until bones snapped and the knife he dropped to the pavement. His opponent didn't make a sound. Nor did he yield. Despite the huge amount of pain he must be suffering, he delivered an uppercut to Bolt's chin that rocked him off his feet.

Dropping to the ground, he swept the man's feet out from under him. And then the two were wrestling, rolling, digging with elbows, gouging with fingers, kneeing exposed shins and thighs.

Despite his useless hand, his opponent put up a remarkable fight. But Bolt found the carotid artery in the man's neck and applied choking pressure until he blacked out. Rolling over, tossing the man's body aside, Bolt began to shove to his feet.

The sound of swishing air warned him, and he ducked. But not fast enough. A crowbar caught him behind the ear. Pain exploded in his head and he fell. The guy with the crushed arm had found it in him to wield the crowbar with his other hand.

The glancing blow almost knocked him out. If he hadn't ducked at the last second his brains and skull would have been spattered among the grease and oil in the parking lot. Blood dripped into his right eye, blurring his vision.

He swiped at his eyes, ordered his feet to gather under him. But his body refused to obey. Shock had set in and it felt as though an electrical cattle prod had zapped him. Pain cramped his muscles but he could hear voices talking.

"Hey. Don't kill him."

"The shithead broke my arm."

No matter how much he willed them to do otherwise, his limbs still wouldn't move.

Bolt heard the click of a hammer being pulled back, signifying a gun about to fire. From this distance, the man couldn't possibly miss.

Amanda, I'm sorry. Sorry I failed to protect you. Sorry that I never told you...

Blackness claimed Bolt.

13

WHEN BOLT HADN'T ARRIVED back at the fashion show's finale, Amanda tried to call him on his cell. He didn't answer. And fifteen minutes later when he still didn't respond, she knew something was very wrong.

Bolt was reliable and as she recalled that loving heat in his eyes, she knew he wouldn't be out of touch unless there was a big problem. She kept telling herself his cell battery could be low, or he could be in a dead area, or changing a flat tire on the rental car, but she wasn't convincing herself. Bolt was too protective and dependable not to call from a pay phone if his cell wasn't working.

Without Bolt to back her, she was uncertain if she could or should proceed. So with trepidation in her heart, she put in a call to Logan Kincaid and wasted no words, coming right to the point. "Bolt isn't answering his cell phone." She gave him the Staten Island garage's address.

Kincaid's calm tone soothed her jangled nerves. "I'll send someone to check on him. And someone to guard you. Don't go back to the apartment—"

"Hathaway expects me to join him at a celebration

party in his suite with the rest of his employees, staff, models and designers." She didn't need to spell out the implications that if she didn't go, Hathaway might be suspicious of her cover.

"There are too many ways he can get you alone."

She was well aware that attending Hathaway's party involved risk, extra risk without Bolt to back her up. But she would never win justice for her sister by playing it safe.

"I'm armed, sir."

"Then it's your call."

She appreciated Kincaid leaving the decision to her. While technically he wasn't her boss, he could easily call her boss and force her hand. Bolt had told her that Kincaid trusted his people in the field, and in turn they gave him their best. She could see why Bolt enjoyed working for the man.

"I need to attend that party."

"Then, I'll try to place one of my people inside with you within an hour."

"Sounds like a plan. And thanks."

She didn't realize security guards stood at the doors with picture identification for each of the guests until after she arrived.

Still, she wasn't unduly alarmed. A man like Kincaid could send someone in with the help.

However, once she stepped inside Hathaway's private lair, she saw that the party was small. His cleaning woman mixed drinks behind the bar and his chef personally passed around the hors d'oeuvres. She'd expected a live band, many more people. Although Hathaway was surrounded by several models and a few staff members, he drilled her with a piercing stare the moment she walked into the room.

And immediately she felt awash in sensuality. She had a sudden yen to kick off her shoes and walk barefoot in the plush carpeting. Her clothes seemed too tight, hugging her most sensitive places. Even her breath came faster, her heart beating with a rhythmic tattoo that made her all too aware of how her hips swayed as she ambled forward.

Perhaps she should have fled but among the others she believed she'd be safe. And then Hathaway shot a myriad of additional fiery sensations her way. And it was as if her body betrayed her. Her breasts swelled, desire ripped through her—despite that she despised Hathaway. Although she'd felt his power before, this time was more unnerving because of the unprecedented intensity of the lust coursing through her veins. Or perhaps it was because Bolt wasn't there to protect her that she felt especially vulnerable.

Hathaway shook off from his arm an auburn-haired supermodel and gestured for Amanda to join him. Her legs trembled and she licked her bottom lip as nerves caught up with her. She decided a quick hello, then pleading a headache and excusing herself was in order.

Hathaway greeted her with a quick embrace, his expression complex. He seemed on top of his game, yet at the same time a bit unsure of himself. "The show went well."

"I thought so."

His smarmy touch and his overpowering cologne should have turned off her lust, but she wasn't that lucky. Her thoughts and genuine feelings seemed to make no difference in her physical reactions. Her nerves were on fire, her gut clenched tight, her blood rushed and made her ears roar.

She tried to take a deep calming breath. She tried to tell herself he wouldn't pull anything in this roomful of people, but she was no longer certain of how far he'd go to attain her. And she began to doubt her ability to protect herself—and her plan to come here at all. Resistance was more than the simple matter of pulling out her gun and telling Hathaway to leave her alone—which would blow her cover.

Get a grip.

It's lust.

You can't die from unfulfilled lust.

But she hadn't known fighting her own needs could be so painful. And when Hathaway grinned the most evil grin she'd ever seen, she realized that he was licking his lips in anticipation of her submission. Mortified, she willed the floor to open up and drop her through it.

Bolt? Where are you?

Why had she dared to come here alone? Because of Donna. Now more than ever, Amanda wanted to prove this man had killed her sister. She wanted him locked up behind bars for the rest of his life.

Anger pushed back some of the sluicing desire, made standing within three feet of Hathaway possible. Yet, she already sensed that anger wasn't enough to keep him away.

"Come."

Hathaway took her arm in the most courteous manner. To anyone else in the room he'd appear the perfect gentleman. But Amanda knew better. She was close enough to see the glint of power in his eyes. Close enough to see the twist of triumph on his lips.

And his superior attitude gave her just enough mental strength to pull back. "I'm sorry. I have a previous engagement. If you'd told me about the party earlier I could have changed my plans."

"For me, you will cancel them now."

He slammed her with a tidal wave of lust. Oh…God.

Her entire body sizzled with unnatural desire. She clenched her gut, braced her feet against the delicious sensations that were rapidly causing her to go mindless.

And when again he took her arm, she didn't have the strength to resist although he was leading her away from the others and through the private doors to his bedroom. She should plant her feet, stop walking. But she seemed to have no control over her muscles. She should have shouted for help. But her vocal cords refused to work.

It was as if he'd washed her body with so much sensation that her mind no longer controlled her actions. Like the victim of a snake's venom she was paralyzed.

She was on her own. If Kincaid had managed to get someone into the party, that person wouldn't have been able to penetrate Hathaway's private bedroom without making a huge scene—especially since Hathaway locked the double doors behind them. He was going to do whatever he wanted with her and she had no way to stop him.

"I've been wanting us to spend time alone together." Hathaway turned to face her with a satisfied leer. "Before the evening is over, you will understand that I always get what I want—and right now what I want is you."

BOLT AWAKENED TO find his wrists and ankles tied behind his back, a gag between his lips, a blindfold over his eyes. From the rocking movement and sound of an engine, he surmised he was in a vehicle. Listening carefully, he noted no other breathing besides his own. Heard no rustling of clothing. Nothing.

Could his captors have been stupid enough to have left him alone? Despite his pounding head, he wasted no time finding out. Stretching his shoulders and arms toward his boot, he released the knife in the hidden compartment of his sole.

Within moments, he was free of his bonds. Ignoring his head wound, which still bled, he took stock of his surroundings. He appeared to be locked in the back of a windowless van. Until they stopped, there wasn't much he could do to escape with only a knife for a weapon. They'd taken his gun and his cell phone.

He tried to put his worry over Amanda aside, but couldn't. He didn't know if he was out of range of the mike she wore, but he couldn't hear her talking. He reached to turn up the volume but his unit was missing. He must have lost it during the fight, or his captors had found it and removed it. He'd told her he'd protect her and now he was too far away to keep his word. That she'd trusted him to keep her safe and he was letting her down hurt more than his head injury. But Bolt wasn't one to anguish over a predicament. He took action. But first he needed a plan. He needed to get to a phone and Amanda as fast as possible.

Obviously Hathaway had wanted to take him out to prevent Bolt from protecting Amanda. So Hathaway must have figured out they were connected, possibly that they weren't who they'd claimed. There could have been any one of numerous slipups—but now was not the time to dwell on how, when or where the mission had gone sour. His primary goal had to be to escape, then find Amanda, whom he was certain was with Hathaway and in trouble.

Usually Bolt could compartmentalize on a mission, set his mind only on the next objective and put his worries aside. Yet, not for one second could he forget that Amanda needed him and he wasn't there for her.

Thinking over his options, he used the blindfold to tie a bandanna tight around his head and hoped the pressure would stop the bleeding. He wished he had some idea of where his captors were taking him. Obviously they had orders to keep him alive or he'd already be dead.

Bolt had two choices. He could sit patiently and attack whomever opened the doors when they arrived at their destination. Surprise would be in his favor. But time might be a critical factor. And for all he knew these people could be driving him across the state.

Bolt's second choice was riskier. He could pound on the sides of the van. The driver might ignore him. Then again, he might not. He might open the door and shoot him.

Bolt leaned forward and placed his ear against the wall separating him from the driver. But he heard nothing except a radio. No conversation.

Did that mean only one man was guarding him? If so that would up his chances of outsmarting or overpowering him. And if he assumed Bolt was still tied and helpless, he might believe one man was enough to keep him prisoner.

Bolt decided the risk was worth a try. He pounded on the cab with his fist to gain the driver's attention. When the van swerved, he realized he'd unnerved the driver. Good.

"Hey, I'm an undercover cop. Let me out." Bolt held his breath. If the driver was the same knife fighter whom he'd previously fought, he doubted the vehicle would even slow or that he'd answer. However, if Bolt had simply been turned over to a low-level thug, the man might not want to stay involved with an officer of the law complicating the situation.

"Shut up."

The accent was pure Long Island. Not the knife fighter's. And a pro wouldn't have responded. Good.

"You're interfering in a joint FBI and police sting. Let me out and I'll put in a good word for you."

"Sure you will."

"You still have my cell phone?"

"You aren't making any calls."

"You make one. And listen to how long it takes to go through. The signal is encrypted. You'll hear the tones scrambling the signal. Dude, you have no idea what you're getting yourself into. You don't need accessory to murder pinned on you." Bolt hoped the man's need for self preservation would overcome his loyalty to whomever had set up the job.

Bolt waited. If the driver didn't have his cell phone, he couldn't take the bait.

Several curses issued from the driver and then he slammed on the brakes. Bolt kept his knife in his hand, but pointed it up his jacket's sleeve.

Would the driver open the door to free him, or shoot him? Or would he simply leave him locked inside and walk away to protect his own hide?

AMANDA HAD NO MEMORY of removing her blouse. Hathaway could have done it or she could have done it herself. She recalled standing there, clenching her teeth, need pouring through her with such intensity that she could barely breathe.

Hathaway was saying something about music, wanting her to dance naked for him. He'd moved to a cabinet beside his headboard and fiddled with his sound system. She didn't recognize the exotic Middle Eastern music but didn't dislike it either. However, she'd never seen such peculiar lighting and it annoyed her.

Hathaway had dimmed all the lights, except one overhead that seemed to be shining right on her, and another that lit up the entire bed like a stage, where Hathaway had propped up the pillows and now leaned back as if he expected her to put on some kind of damn show. This couldn't be happening. She shouldn't be here. But trapped by a body that betrayed her, she couldn't leave.

His power was unnatural. Irresistible. And she began to sway her hips in a sensual motion without any further prodding from him. He'd likely done the same thing to dozens of other women, and she'd been a fool to think she was strong enough to resist.

Her feet moved to the tempo, and her shoulders seemed to shimmy of their own accord. Damn the man. It was as if he were a puppet master pulling her strings and she was helpless to do anything except exactly what he so obviously desired.

No. She didn't want to remove her bra. Yet her hands raised to the fasteners and not only did she seductively shrug it off, she circled it over her head and flung it at Hathaway. And then she danced for him, her blood boiling, her anger no weapon against his malevolent desire.

"The skirt," he demanded, his voice hoarse with satisfaction. "Remove it."

God, help her. If she removed her skirt, he'd see the gun fastened to her thigh. Her cover would be blown. She couldn't. She wouldn't. But her hands unzipped the skirt. Her hips shimmied and Hathaway actually clapped as she stood before him in her panties, gun and heels.

His gaze rested on the gun. "You're just full of interesting surprises." And then he leered. "And you're going to pay for every one."

She told her hand to reach for the gun and shoot the son of a bitch, but her muscles refused to obey. Instead she danced, her hips swaying, her gun on her thigh mocking her inability to take action.

"Don't think Timmins will save you, either. Although he may arrive in time to watch the denouement."

"Huh?"

"He's on his way here, trussed up like a Thanksgiving Day turkey and he's going to watch you beg me to take you. And when I do, your scream of satisfaction will be the last thing he ever hears."

Bolt? He was going to kill Bolt?

Bolt had given up the perfume bottle to help her find Donna's killer. She wasn't going to let him die.

Fear like she had never known took hold of her and clamped over her heart. She didn't know if Hathaway's use of the unnatural power from the perfume bottle had caused him to become unbalanced or if he'd always been that way. But she did know that she'd rather die than let him kill Bolt.

And that's when she knew. She loved Bolt. And despite her fear for him, despite what Hathaway had planned with his evil conniving, she focused on her love for Bolt. Of all the stupid times to figure it out, now had to be the worst.

She might never get to tell him.

BOLT CROUCHED in the vehicle, his every muscle ready to spring forward into a diving roll. Metal squealed as the driver threw back a latch.

The door cracked open and Bolt struck the panel with both feet. His momentum carried him outside into the night and knocked down a man he assumed was the driver. He landed on weeds and grass where the driver had pulled off the road.

When he recovered from the roll in the slippery grass, he came up with his knife in hand, prepared to throw it if necessary. But the driver hadn't moved. And a quick check showed that he was breathing, but unconscious. Bolt hefted the driver into the van and bolted the door.

The keys were still in the ignition, his cell phone on the seat. One glance and he realized the driver had been taking him back into the city. Just a short drive through the tunnel and he'd be back in Manhattan. Slipping into the driver's seat, he started the engine, picked up the phone and called Amanda. When she didn't answer, Bolt tried Kincaid who filled him in.

Just as he suspected, Hathaway had Amanda in his suite. Although she'd made it clear to Kincaid that she intended to stay in a group, she hadn't known that Hathaway had set up Bolt.

Kincaid hadn't yet been able to get a man into the suite, but Bolt would get there first anyway. His pulse accelerated.

Bolt floored the gas pedal.

Hold on, Amanda. I'm coming.

AMANDA HELD ON to the thought of how much she loved Bolt. Her newfound love for him comforted her. Made her stronger.

Hathaway's hold on her seemed to lessen as she focused on Bolt. Maybe she was distracting her mind from the truth, but as she remembered Bolt's gentle touch, as she recalled how wonderful he'd been to her right from the start, she seemed able to resist dancing closer to that bed.

She recalled Bolt's willingness to let her set the pace. He'd even waited on his knees for her in the bathtub to help give her back her self-esteem. The man had been nothing but heroic. And she was certain he was doing everything he could to get back to her now. Bolt wouldn't give up. Not on her. Not on their mission.

Hathaway gestured for her to come closer to the bed, and for the moment, her body didn't betray her. She maintained her distance. Hathaway grimaced, his lips tightening into a repulsive frown of disapproval, and he sent a new deluge of lust at her.

She countered by focusing on how much she loved Bolt. He was out there somewhere. She could feel his presence warming her heart and fueling her resolve. She imagined his love as a cozy fleece blanket wrapped around her, reinforcing her determination to resist Hathaway.

And it was working. She didn't understand how.

Anger hadn't made a dent in Hathaway's powers. But her love for Bolt helped her hold her own.

However, from the sweat pouring down Hathaway's ruddy cheeks, he must have sensed that his powers weren't working as he expected. Not about to accept defeat, he curled his lips into a feral grin. "You won't escape."

"Is that what you told Donna?" Amanda made a stab at acquiring the answers she so badly wanted. Perhaps the combination of Hathaway's arrogance and his agitated state would cause him to reveal what had happened to her sister.

"I killed the bitch and I'll kill you. After you please me, of course."

She'd always suspected Hathaway had committed murder, but to hear him admit it so coldly and calculatingly caused her to falter. He had killed Donna. He'd taken her sister's life, preventing her from ever marrying, having children. Amanda had lost her last living relative.

For a moment Amanda thought she might be sick.

She reminded herself that Bolt's love would get her through this. And with Hathaway so frustrated by her refusal to succumb, now was her opportunity to get answers. But she had to be careful. She couldn't allow him to distract her because failing to concentrate on Bolt's love was like letting down a shield and Hathaway's evil would arrow through.

And despite Hathaway's admission. She still had no proof.

"Why did you kill my sister?"

Hathaway's eyes widened in surprise and then he laughed. "Your sister?"

"Yes. Why did—"

"I offered her a world of power. All she had to do was replicate a special potion—but she refused. And then she started to stir up trouble—"

"So you got rid of the troublemaker?"

"Exactly."

His admission burned through Amanda like a white-hot knife. But that anger cost her. She took two steps that had advanced her to the foot of the bed.

She had to banish her anger and concentrate on why she loved Bolt. She recalled how he always believed in her. And how when she gave in to Hathaway's powers, he never cast blame. Knowing Bolt wouldn't blame her for that two-step lapse made it easier to forgive herself.

"However, if I'd known about you, I might have kept your sister alive a little longer. I've never had sisters."

She had Hathaway's measure now. He was trying to cause her to lose focus. But she held on to the memory of Bolt, his quiet confidence, his gentle touch, his sensual caresses and his spicy kisses.

And took a step back.

Then two.

Hathaway clenched his hands into fists. But his surge of energy wasn't forcing her to go to him. She even scooped up her shirt and shrugged it on.

"The bottle won't help you," she taunted him. "Not this time."

"Did your sister give you an antidote?"

Bolt had. Her love for him was protecting her. He might not be there beside her, but he was with her in spirit.

Hathaway pointed at her, his steely tone, demanding and commanding. "I'm tired of talking. Tired of playing games. You will come to me. Right now."

He deluged her with sensation.

She fought back. "The only reason I'm here is to ensure you go to jail. I'm certainly not climbing into your bed."

Her refusal caused his face to turn purple. For a moment she thought he might have a stroke or a heart attack, but she wasn't that lucky.

Hathaway had finally realized he wouldn't win their mental battle. So like the lowlife he was, he tried to cheat by lunging for her.

For a heavy man, he moved with surprising quickness and agility. But Amanda was no longer paralyzed. Hathaway came at her, arms stretched, fingers clasping for her throat.

Reaching for her gun, she slapped her palm on the handle and drew the weapon from the holster. She raised the gun. Aimed. Fired.

Hathaway collapsed at her feet, a bloody hole in his shoulder, his hand clasping the wound. "You bitch. I'll have you arrested for attempted murder."

She kept the gun pointed at him. But she began to shake. She'd never shot anyone before and horror rose up her throat. She'd just shot a man in cold blood. Without proof that Hathaway had killed Donna, her claim of self-defense might not stand up in court.

Her numb fingers let the gun drop to the floor. As Hathaway's party guests pounded on the locked bedroom door, she realized they'd heard her fire the shot. She dressed quickly, then called 911.

14

BOLT HEARD THE GUNSHOT and sprinted into Hathaway's suite. A cluster of panicked staff and models stood milling outside the double bedroom doors. A Shey Group agent had just picked the bedroom door's lock and Bolt grabbed the knob.

"Keep everyone out," he ordered the other agent.

The agent nodded and placed himself in front of the doors. Bolt slipped inside. And Amanda flung herself at him. He caught her in a giant bear hug, his heart lightening with relief. "Are you all right?"

"I shot him. I shot Hathaway." Then she burst into tears.

He held tight to her shaking body. "You're going to be fine."

"He admitted he killed Donna. He told me he'd do the same to me." She wiped away her tears with her fingers. "We have to prove it was self-defense or I'm going to jail for attempted murder."

Hathaway inched across the floor, leaving a trail of blood. Bolt glared at Hathaway, who stopped moving. "If he's dead, he can't lie anymore."

Amanda drew several deep breaths to steady herself

and then pulled away, a new strength in her eyes. "Instead of killing him, perhaps you could get him to tell us where his diary is."

Hathaway shook his head. "What diary?"

Bolt released her and strode toward Hathaway. At his advance, Hathaway passed out, whether from fear or lack of blood Bolt didn't know. However, he didn't trust him and used a drapery cord to tie his hands behind his back. Then he wound a belt around his arm to stop the bleeding.

The paramedics would arrive soon. Cops would follow. They needed answers or Amanda would be in trouble. And a man as powerful as Hathaway could pull strings. To protect Amanda, he really needed proof of Hathaway's guilt. As much as he would have liked to shoot Hathaway again, he couldn't kill a defenseless man. But what that decision might do to Amanda was tearing Bolt apart.

She paced like a caged tigress. "I still want to find that diary. I want the evidence to prove his evil to the entire world, or I can't clear Donna's name. I haven't forgotten how her patent was discovered on a terrorist's computer. He must have killed her and then sold it for profit as an added bonus." How typical that she was thinking about her sister more than herself. Amanda frowned. "I didn't tell you—according to Hathaway, Donna refused to work on a chemical formula for the perfume." She looked thoughtful for a moment. "Hathaway also asked me how I resisted him. He asked if I had an antidote."

"Donna must have figured out an antidote—that's why Hathaway killed her," Bolt said, finishing her thought.

Bolt noticed that while Amanda seemed to have regrouped, she faced away from Hathaway's unconscious body. But she wasn't asking Bolt to take her away from there—she still wanted to find the diary.

And he would not let her down. The police sirens in front of the building suddenly complicated matters. He took out his cell phone and made a quick call to Kincaid. "I need police cooperation."

"You'll have it," Kincaid promised.

Bolt turned to Amanda. "I want you to tell the police everything. And we're going to see if they'll help us find that diary. But before they get here, there's one thing I want to know."

"What?"

"How did you resist Hathaway?"

"I found out by accident that a certain strong emotion could counter the bottle's effect."

"What emotion?"

"Every time I thought about you, Hathaway's power weakened. My love for you kept me safe." Her eyes sparkled and his heart pounded with happiness.

She loved him. He wanted to sweep her out of the room, take her across the street to a place without an unconscious body, without homicide detectives, where he could have her all to himself. But that would take hours.

She loved him.

He took her into his arms for a kiss. That was how the cops would have found them, liplocked, except for a disturbance at the bedroom door.

The Shey Agent was refusing to let the cops pass. Damn. "It's okay. Let them in," Bolt called out, annoyed he'd forgotten such a detail. But his thoughts couldn't quite wrap around the fact that Amanda loved him. For a while there, she seemed so determined to keep her feelings reined in tight that he wondered if she'd ever love him. And now that she did, he was so happy he wanted to laugh and shout it to the world. Not exactly appropriate behavior considering the circumstances.

He needed to find the damn diary for her or the woman he loved might spend the rest of her life in jail.

At his bidding, the cops helped. They turned the suite upside down. But they found nothing.

As his hopes began to dim, Amanda's back straightened, her lips pressed together with determination. She wasn't giving up.

Remembering the secret panel in the walk-in closet, Bolt returned to retrieve the stolen perfume bottle, which the Shey Group would now return to its rightful owner. Before he'd found the secret compartment in the wall, Bolt had noted other irregularities, but he hadn't explored further after he'd found the bottle.

But now, he worked slowly. His fingers inched along the wooden paneling and he closed his eyes to concentrate on discrepancies. Frustrated when he failed to find anything, he headed back into the bedroom to find Amanda staring hard at the ceiling light, the paramedics taking care of Hathaway, who still hadn't come to.

"What is it?"

"Hathaway had this room lit like a stage. That light—" she pointed over the bed "—was turned on to its brightest setting." She moved to a place about three feet in front of the bed. "He had another bright light on me and the rest of the room was dark."

"And?"

"He'd set the lighting as if he intended to film his bedroom activities. Maybe we shouldn't be searching for a diary. Maybe he used a camcorder to record his activities."

"There's an entire cabinet of DVDs. Let's look more closely." Bolt opened the nightstand cabinet and searched the titles. He recognized most of the movies. "Nothing unusual here."

Amanda opened a case, popped a disk into the DVD player and turned on the television. An orgy filled the screen. A private orgy recorded in full surround sound and high digital color, within the confines of Hathaway's home. Bolt recognized a few of the models, Hathaway in the center of things. It wasn't the proof they needed, but perhaps somewhere in the stack of DVDs might be a clue.

A detective assured them that his men would carefully go through every DVD. And Bolt was glad Amanda wouldn't have to watch them. She'd been through enough.

He took her back across the street and they showered, then lounged together in the giant tub and tried to ignore the cop who'd followed them to make certain they didn't try to leave. Cooperation between the Shey Group and the police only went so far. Bolt ordered pizza delivered. And by mutual consent they stuck to small talk. Both needed time to unwind.

When the phone rang and the homicide detective's

name came up on caller ID, Bolt put the call on speakerphone so Amanda could listen. "We found what you needed, Mr. Tanner. One of the DVDs showed Hathaway shooting Donna Lane. Right on the DVD he tells her his plan to steal her patent and sell it to the highest bidder. He says it's payback for her creating an antidote and trying to ruin him."

"Thanks." Bolt hung up, the pressure in his chest lightening. Amanda wasn't going to jail. Hathaway was. At the joy of knowing he had all the time in the world to spend with her, he felt like dancing.

"So your theory was correct." Amanda leaned forward and kissed Bolt on the cheek.

"I'm always correct," he teased. "Haven't you learned that yet?"

She smacked her hand against her forehead, but laughter escaped her lips. "You were certainly right about me."

"And what's that?"

"We're good together."

"Yes, we are." She'd seemed to have gone from uncertain if they had a future together straight to love. And he was right there with her. They might not have known one another long, but he looked forward to their spending a lot of time together. "I was thinking about moving."

"Moving?" She cocked her brow. "I don't know even where you live. Come to think of it, there's quite a lot I don't know about you."

"You know the important stuff. And I was thinking

Florida is too far away. So I'm going to move so we can be closer."

"To New Jersey."

"How about I move in with you?"

She laughed again. "You'd give up your home to live with me?"

"There isn't much I wouldn't give up for you. Amanda, I love you."

of his family. They wanted to visit places and mother
as soon as possible. Amanda even seemed amiable and
the danger was behind them all and his life with
wife's family of... at the important things... like the
important things... like the world she adored and kissed her

Epilogue

Bolt moved into Amanda's home one week later.
Amanda had visited Donna's grave and seemed to have
made peace with the past. With Hathaway in jail without bond, the evidence against him solid and the perfume bottle returned to its rightful owner, the case was
completed.

The police had found proof that Hathaway was responsible for the accident that had ruined Melanie's career and she could collect enough from his estate to live
comfortably for the rest of her life. The danger was behind them all and his life with Amanda was before him.

In many ways, he and Amanda didn't know one another that well. He hadn't realized that she adored eating
popcorn and chocolate in bed while she watched late-
night movies. Or that she loved to paint landscapes, or
that she enjoyed yoga. However, he knew the important
things—like the courage with which she faced the world.

She'd found the courage to lose control of her emotions around him. And he vowed always to make it safe
for her to do so.

And he'd learned that she was eager to become part

of his family. She wanted to visit his sisters and mother as soon as possible. Amanda even adored children and the idea of starting a family appealed as much to her as it did to him.

She'd never again feel alone and unloved. Bolt would make certain of it.

And as he brought her breakfast in bed and kissed her awake, he didn't think he'd ever tire of watching her open her eyes with a bright curiosity to face the day—well, at least after a strong cup of coffee. He set the tray beside the bed and kissed her lips. "Wake up, sleepyhead."

"Mmm." She wrapped her arms around his neck and opened her green eyes, which reminded him of the sea on a windy day. "You smell like cherry jelly and coffee."

"Breakfast awaits."

She snuggled against him. "You're spoiling me."

"I have a secret motive."

"Not so secret." She trailed a hand down his chest and his stomach to his erection. "I'm so glad you moved in."

"Me, too."

She glanced into his eyes, joy shining through. "I've never been happier."

Her simple words warmed him straight to his heart. "Good. I plan to keep it that way."

"Really?"

"Uh-huh." His mouth angled to capture hers. "Because my love for you is uncontrollable."

HARLEQUIN® *Blaze*™

Where were you when the lights went out?

Shane Walker was seducing his best friend in:

#194 NIGHT MOVES

by **Julie Kenner** July 2005

Adam and Mallory were rekindling
the flames of first love in:

#200 WHY NOT TONIGHT?

by **Jacquie D'Alessandro** August 2005

Simon Thackery was professing his love...
to his best friend's fiancée in:

#206 DARING IN THE DARK

by **Jennifer LaBrecque** September 2005

24 Hours:
BLÆCKOUT

presents
the final installment of

*The Reilly triplets bet they could go
ninety days without sex. Hmm.*

THE LAST
REILLY STANDING
by Maureen Child

(SD #1664, available July 2005)

Aidan Reilly was determined to win the bet
he'd made with his brothers. Three months
without sex meant one thing: spend *a lot* of
time with his best gal pal Terry Evans. She had
given up on love long ago because the pain
just wasn't worth it. Then…temptation proved
to be too much. The last Reilly standing had
lost the bet, but could he win the girl?

Available at your favorite retail outlet.

If you enjoyed what you just read,
then we've got an offer you can't resist!

Take 2 bestselling
love stories FREE!
Plus get a FREE surprise gift!

HARLEQUIN® *Blaze*™

New York Times bestselling author

Elizabeth Bevarly

answers the question

Can men and women have sex and still be friends?

with

INDECENT SUGGESTION
Blaze #189

Best friends Becca and Turner try hypnosis
to kick their smoking habit...instead, they get
the uncontrollable urge to burn up the sheets!
Doesn't that make them more than friends?

Be sure to catch this funny,
sexy story available in July 2005!